CIRCLE OF BLOOD BOOK SIX:

LOVERS' VICTORY

Other books by R. A. Steffan

The Last Vampire: Book One
The Last Vampire: Book Two
The Last Vampire: Book Three
The Last Vampire: Book Four
The Last Vampire: Book Five
The Last Vampire: Book Six

Vampire Bound: Book One
Vampire Bound: Book Two
Vampire Bound: Book Three
Vampire Bound: Book Four

Forsaken Fae: Book One
Forsaken Fae: Book Two
Forsaken Fae: Book Three

The Sixth Demon: Book One
The Sixth Demon: Book Two
The Sixth Demon: Book Three

The Complete Horse Mistress Collection
The Complete Lion Mistress Collection
The Complete Dragon Mistress Collection
The Complete Master of Hounds Collection

Antidote: Love and War, Book 1
Antigen: Love and War, Book 2
Antibody: Love and War, Book 3
Anthelion: Love and War, Book 4
Antagonist: Love and War, Book 5

LOVERS' VICTORY

R. A. STEFFAN & JAELYNN WOOLF

INTRODUCTION

This book contains graphic violence and explicit sexual content. It is intended for a mature audience.

TABLE OF CONTENTS

ONE

The entrance to the ancient Egyptian compound of Saqqara was simultaneously claustrophobic and overwhelming. It was narrower than Amy had pictured, but the fluted stone columns rising on either side of her loomed like giants in the shadows. She hoisted her backpack more comfortably on her shoulders and slanted a glance at Elijah, feeling a sudden bout of nervousness.

"I can't believe you used to come here for work every day," she said. "Why on earth did you give it up?"

Both she and her husband boasted the title of 'Doctor' before their names, but in Elijah's case, it was a PhD in Archaeology to go along with his Master's in Cultural Anthropology. To say that Amy's doctorate was a little more mundane was putting it mildly.

Elijah shot her a sideways glance, his mahogany eyes flat and expressionless, as they so often seemed to be these days. "It's a pile of dusty rocks and sand, Ames. When you've picked through a few dozen places like this for weeks at a time under the desert sun, they start to lose their appeal," he said. His jaw worked, a tendon standing out under his dark skin. "Which isn't to say I'm thrilled about a bunch of hippies camping here and destroying the place. The regular tourist crowds are hard enough on historical sites."

Back home in Pennsylvania, Elijah was a professor at West Parklands University. For the first few years of their relationship, he had been passionate about going on digs all over the world, and he'd been part of the team working on the restoration of the very site they were walking through. These days, Amy was lucky to get her husband to take her out for dinner and a movie.

She suspected he was suffering from clinical depression and had been for some time, but on the handful of occasions she'd brought it up, Elijah had brushed her off. And lately, things in the world at large were becoming so hopelessly whacked that the idea of badgering someone into therapy because they no longer felt fulfilled by their job seemed… shallow, somehow.

Not to mention the fact that if he did submit to getting help, any psychologist worth his or her salt would want to drag Amy in as well for joint counseling. Which… wasn't something she was in much of a hurry to do.

Hypocrisy for the win.

So, instead, here they were—half a world away from home, hanging out with the hippies while rioting and border wars flared in countries around the globe. She ran a hand over her belly absently.

"Let's just get inside the complex and check things out," she said, painfully aware that Elijah had only agreed to this trip to humor her. From the look of things, he was regretting the decision more and more by the minute.

"Yeah. Okay." His tone was flat, but a moment later, his fingers brushed hers. She tangled their hands together gratefully, the creamy white of her skin contrasting with the rich dark brown of his.

They'd always been a study in opposites. Amy's genes came straight from Ireland—she was pale and freckled with curly red hair and green eyes. Elijah was more than a head taller than her, a devastatingly handsome black man with close-cropped hair and an athlete's build. Indeed, he'd been a marathon runner when she'd first met him—another passion of his that had fallen by the wayside over the years.

Coming here to Saqqara had become a strange obsession for Amy. In the last few weeks, reports had started appearing on the internet—communes spontaneously popping up at spiritual and cultural sites across the world. She couldn't really explain her desire to come to this place; certainly, there were several other sites closer to their home. Maybe it was because Saqqara had been the first such enclave to appear. Maybe it was because Elijah had been here before.

Whatever the case, something about the gathering of people at Saqqara called to her. It was totally irrational, but a part of her mind insisted that here, she and Elijah might find the part of their lives that had been missing. The part that was slowly destroying them with its absence.

She stifled a snort. She could almost hear Elijah saying, *"Don't be ridiculous. All you'll find here is an increased risk of skin cancer and, if you're not careful, a bout of gastroenteritis."*

4

Bright light made Amy's eyes water as they reached the end of the claustrophobic stone corridor and stepped into a massive, open esplanade.

Amy's eyes widened at the sight beyond. It was completely different than what she had expected. Overwhelming, like the first time she saw the ocean as a child. Seeing places like this on television or in books simply couldn't convey the awe-inspiring size of them.

"This is… *wow*. Amazing." She placed her hand above her eyes, shielding them from the glare of the unforgiving desert sun. Her gaze took in the wall of the southern tomb, a row of cobra heads carved along the top as though standing guard over the space below. To their right, some distance away, stood the step pyramid. "Oh, my god. This is *so damned cool*. How tall is that thing?"

"Sixty-two meters. About two hundred feet," Elijah said. His attention wasn't on the pyramid or the cobra head wall, however. It was on the incredible bustle of human activity filling this ancient place. "So many people," he whispered, shaking his head. "This was a terrible idea."

Amy winced, and tried to cover it. Who knew five words could hurt so much?

She whirled on her husband and pulled her hand free from his, schooling her voice to stay low and even. "You said you'd try. Thanks *so much* for the ten minutes of effort you just expended. It must have been excruciating to endure."

A frown drew his brows together. "I didn't mean coming here. I meant… *this*." He gestured at the space filled with tents and portaloos and solar panels and power cables and people. "Look at it! These idiots could ruin all the work archaeologists put into restoring this place."

Relief combined with a momentary feeling of sheepishness deflated her bubble of anger. Damned if she'd show it, though.

"Well, it doesn't look like they're ruining it to me," Amy said stubbornly. She returned her gaze to the crowd of people gathered in the shadow of the pyramid. The atmosphere was peaceful as they chatted amiably or rested against the rough stone. "Besides, I think it's wonderful, all these people coming together. Standing up for something."

"Couldn't they have stood up for something while staying at—I don't know—a convention center, or a hotel or something?" Elijah muttered. "They could have gone to the Luxor in Vegas if they thought the whole 'pyramid' vibe was so important."

"No, it wouldn't be the same," Amy said, taking in the aura of peace that covered the ancient site like a comforting blanket. "There's something about this place, don't you think? It feels… powerful, yet calm."

Elijah blew out a breath. "Sorry—I don't feel anything but annoyed. They're turning this site into a joke. I mean, come on. Portable toilets at the base of the oldest pyramid in Egypt?"

She stopped herself from asking if he'd rather the people here used the sand dunes as a great big human litter box instead. Bickering wouldn't help the situation. It never did. God knew they'd tested *that* theory often enough over the past few years.

"There's still something about it," she insisted. "Something I can't quite put my finger on." She took a deep breath of the hot dry air and let it out slowly, closing her eyes. "It feels like... like a weight's been lifted from me. Like something inside me is lighter. Everything just seems... familiar. You have to at least admit that."

She opened her eyes to find Elijah looking down at her with a raised eyebrow. "Yes, I admit—it's familiar. That's probably because I've been here before."

Amy wrinkled her nose at him, coming to terms with the fact that this trip wouldn't be as smooth and easy a feat as she might have hoped. *Please, let this excursion not have been the stupidest idea I've ever had,* she prayed to whatever ancient gods might be lingering around this place.

Her plaintive prayer was interrupted by the approach of a lovely olive-skinned woman. She looked Indian, or perhaps Pakistani. Her waist-length black hair hung in a silken wave down her back, and her hazelnut eyes were depthless, full of a haunting sadness.

Still, her gaze was direct and assessing as she looked them over. She lifted her chin and offered them a brief, soft smile that didn't touch her grief-filled eyes.

"My name is Manisha," she said. "Welcome to the Saqqara necropolis."

TWO

From the moment Elijah stepped onto the tarmac at Cairo's airport, he'd had this strange sense that something pivotal—and potentially devastating—was about to happen in his and Amy's lives. It wasn't his damned depression talking, either. At least, he was fairly sure it wasn't. An off-kilter pressure had taken root within his chest, and as much as he tried to ignore it, there it continued to sit like one of the ancient sandstone blocks from Djoser's pyramid.

Maybe it was a ridiculous thing to think, but the woman who'd appeared to greet them at the entrance to the esplanade looked like someone carrying around a similar weight, despite her pleasant smile as she greeted them in lightly accented English.

Amy smiled back and reached out a hand. "Nice to meet you. I'm Dr. Amy Carpenter, and this is my husband, Elijah."

The woman—Manisha— shook hands with Amy and lifted her eyebrows. "Americans, eh? Where in the States are you from?"

"East Coast. Pennsylvania, to be specific," Amy said. "My husband is actually an archaeology professor. He's been here on digs before."

His wife's smile lit up her green eyes. She always sounded so proud of Elijah's accomplishments, even though he'd not added all that many since they got married and he stopped making career moves.

"Very good. So you know the area, then?" Manisha asked.

Elijah cleared his throat. "A bit, yes. Though I have to say I've never seen the place looking quite like this before," he muttered, his scowl returning as he once more took in the controlled chaos around them.

Manisha did not appear to notice his testy tone. "There are many people here seeking refuge from the upheaval in the world, and they need access to the basics like power, water, and sanitation. We're using composting toilets and recycling as much of our graywater as we can capture. The solar panels are a way to access the earth's resources without putting more strain on it."

Elijah pursed his lips.

"You disagree with that?" Manisha raised an eyebrow in mild challenge, or possibly amusement.

His irritation surged. "No. It's just… this place. It's an irreplaceable historical site."

"We understand that. Don't worry, Dr. Carpenter. When the threat to the world has passed, this site will be restored to its previous condition."

"'The threat to the world,'" Elijah echoed flatly.

The woman still didn't rise to his bait. "Just so. As I was saying, many people have come to Saqqara seeking refuge from the upheaval around them. We're happy to have you and your wife, but there are rules you must adhere to in order to keep peace amongst the visitors."

Beneath his tension, Elijah felt terrible. After all, he had promised Amy he would make an actual effort during this trip and yet something about the place still felt... disquieting.

Disquieting? That's the best you can come up with? Great. All those years of higher education certainly paid off, didn't they? Elijah let out a sigh, shaking his head at himself.

If he wasn't careful, his attitude was going to ruin everything. This trip obviously meant a lot to Amy, and he *had* made her a promise. The least he could do was be here for her instead of expending his mental effort on irrational, non-existent emotional perceptions. He wasted enough energy on that kind of shit at home.

Elijah loved his wife more than anything in the world. Still, he couldn't seem to shake the feeling that something bad loomed on the horizon—that leaving Pennsylvania and coming here to Saqqara wouldn't be the refuge Amy was seeking. It felt more like jumping from the frying pan straight into the flames of hell.

Stop, he admonished himself once more, growling silently at his apparent inability not to act like an asshole. Elijah had no intention of losing his wife, damn it. Not now. Not ever.

Yes, strange things were going on around the world, but nothing supernatural like the panic-mongers had started saying. Science and reason could explain everything that was happening, from the riots to the radiation sickness, and he was confident he could prove that to Amy as well. He just needed to *talk* to her instead of arguing or sniping at her.

He rubbed at the stubble that had begun growing on his chin. He'd not had the chance to shave since leaving the states. Maybe he could use time here to revive his career? And perhaps save his marriage at the same time. But the sad truth was, it would take science and reason to save the world, not hippies and whatever new age, feel good crap Amy was hoping to find in this place.

"Rules?" he said, recalling himself to the conversation. "Of course. That makes sense. You'll have to excuse my lack of manners. I'm afraid I'm pretty jet-lagged."

The look that Manisha gave him was a bit too penetrating. A bit too knowing. It only added to his sense of being off-balance, and his jaw clenched.

"I was saying that you and your wife may move freely around the encampment, speak to others and get a feel for the area," she said. "Some come here only to decide it wasn't what they were expecting, so we suggest you take a day or two before determining whether you'd like to stay longer or not."

Amy and Elijah hadn't really discussed how long they planned to stay. This was likely due to Elijah's reluctance to discuss much of anything these days, especially when it was almost certain to end in a fight. Manisha made a good point, though. And if Elijah still felt this irrational sense of foreboding after getting more of a feel for the place, it could be an easy way out for him.

"That's a good idea, right, Amy? We'll give it a day, and decide then if we want to stay longer?" Elijah looked to his wife, who was already showing signs of disappointment.

"I suppose." The smile that had briefly graced her full lips faded.

The emptiness that seemed to have taken up permanent residence in Elijah's stomach grew deeper. No matter how hard he tried, he felt like a perpetual disappointment to his wife. He reminded himself again why he'd come here in the first place… to try and save their marriage.

"I'm not saying I definitely want to leave tomorrow," he said. "I made you a promise, after all."

Amy's eyes rose to his, and the tentative smile returned. "Thank you."

"Well, then," Manisha said. "You're free to find a shady space and set up camp. Many people here speak English. We only have a few rules. No stealing. No violence. People come here seeking refuge from the dangers outside. They don't need any more drama than they're already experiencing. Treat others as you'd like them to treat you; common courtesy is expected by all."

"That's no problem," Amy said. "If everyone could abide by those rules, we wouldn't be in this mess in the first place, right?"

If everyone could abide by those rules, humanity would be a very different species than it is, Elijah thought, but kept his mouth shut.

"Very true," Manisha replied. "We have tents set up over there." She pointed at a pair of large, colorful tents at the far end of the esplanade. "You will find food and water inside, and further down, behind the green tent, sanitary facilities. Please, make yourself at home, Amy. Elijah." She extended her hand first to Amy, then to him. When he took it, her grip was cool and firm as she continued, "If you need anything, ask around. Someone will point you in the right direction."

With a final sad smile, she moved past Amy and Elijah to meet more new arrivals entering the compound behind them.

"Thank you, Elijah," Amy said quietly. "I know you don't really want to be here, and I do appreciate your efforts."

"I made you a promise. I'm going to keep it." Elijah grasped her hand in his again, and she let him.

With a deep breath, he took another slow look around the area. There were many smaller tents set up in addition to the large ones Manisha had pointed out—close to a hundred lined up in the shadows of the archaic walls, he thought. Most appeared occupied, their inhabitants likely waiting out the brutal daytime desert temperatures.

Elijah wondered if the solar panels were hooked into a battery system to give the place nighttime lighting. In fairness, solar panels did make a good amount of sense in a land where the sun was so unrelenting. If they had to make alterations to meet the needs of the visitors here, solar energy was probably the least invasive way of doing so.

"Let's stake out a spot," Amy suggested, pulling Elijah along the stone-lined walkway by their joined hands. After a few minutes, they found a suitable place in a somewhat shady area and set up camp.

It had been years since Elijah had camped in conditions like these, and Amy wasn't usually the outdoorsy type, so it wasn't something they were used to doing together. That was part of the reason why it had surprised him so much when she expressed interest in coming here in the first place. He wondered if, after a day or two of roughing it in hundred-degree heat, Amy might be ready to return to their comfortable house back in the States. They'd spent so much time planning their dream home and having it built after they got married. Who would have thought once they finally moved in, everything between them would start to fall apart?

THREE

After setting up their tent, Amy suggested that they check out the food and water situation, then rest in the shade until things started to cool off a bit.

We could rest now," Elijah countered, eyeing her drawn features. "We've still got plenty of bottled water and energy bars in the packs."

Amy shaded her eyes and peered at the afternoon sun, then glanced at her pale arms, which were already starting to redden despite the sunscreen she'd applied. "I guess so," she said. "I do want to explore later, though."

"Aren't you tired?" Elijah asked, as they pulled out drinks and settled in the shade by the tent. "You didn't sleep much on the flight, I thought you might want to nap until nightfall."

"Yeah, I'm definitely a bit frazzled," she admitted, "but I'm also way too wired to sleep right now, I'm afraid."

Elijah made himself as comfortable as he could, opening the bottle of water and chugging half of it. He thought of all the places he'd rather be than here in the desert, hot as hell and sweating like a sinner in a summer revival tent.

Amy was looking around the place with an expression of fascination, clearly excited to be here despite her fatigue. Meanwhile, Elijah could barely peel the scowl off his face. Sometimes, it felt like that scowl had been permanently etched into his features for the past three years.

Coming back to this site was not having the effect on him Amy had probably hoped it would. All Elijah felt right now was a sort of dull self-loathing at everything he'd failed to accomplish in recent years, both in his professional and personal life.

You gave this up, said the ugly inner voice that delighted in pointing out his shortcomings. *And for what?*

After he'd married Amy, he went on a few digs—both here in Egypt, and elsewhere. When he came home, though, Amy always seemed distant. Elijah eventually decided to give up archaeological expeditions in favor of spending more time with his wife. It worked—for a while, at least.

Then Amy started pulling away again. She'd find all of these different causes to volunteer for. Charity events. Things that were undeniably noble, but that took her away from him.

While Amy was out trying to make a difference in the world, Elijah became more closed off. He'd stopped writing papers, and for a university-level professor in the sciences, that was a problem. An academic who didn't do research had little chance of climbing the professional ladder. Fortunately, he'd already gotten tenure shortly before they married... but the warnings still came. Given the way academia was changing, he was skating on thin ice after years of career stagnation—tenure or no.

The thought of doing some research while he was here had crossed his mind. In fact, that's how he'd managed to get time off to come in the first place—by convincing the head of the archeology department he'd have a research project ready to publish in the spring semester.

It could well be his last chance to avoid losing his job. And that was another thing he really didn't want to tell Amy.

Elijah sat, silently cataloguing the damage he'd done to their future. Predictably, the more he stewed, the more irritated and emotional he got. He glanced at Amy sitting beside him. The enchanted expression on her face as she watched their surroundings just made him feel worse. Following her gaze, he tried to figure out what, precisely, she was staring at.

Across the esplanade from them, a woman who looked to be about nineteen sat between two young men, her arms linked with each of theirs. They were laughing. Talking. Happy.

Two men, both doting on the girl like she was the only woman in the world.

How the hell could they all be so happy when the world was falling down around them? Didn't they *get it*? There were no happy endings in this life.

Amy was still watching them, her features growing wistful. Something about it made a hot, hard lump rise in Elijah's chest. Weren't things hard enough for just two people? He tried to rationalize it. The trio obviously wasn't blood-related, but they could be college buddies. Maybe the guys were gay and she was just their friend. Maybe they were competing for her, and things would turn ugly once she chose between them. Maybe—

"What's wrong?" Amy was staring at him now, rather than the laughing threesome. Whatever she saw on his face made her narrow her eyes. Her lips thinned.

Elijah looked around at all the people. The place really did look like a hippie camp. What the hell had Amy been thinking that made her want to come here?

His thoughts overflowed into words without his conscious decision. "Look at this place. Amy, this is crazy. Seriously. Why are we here?"

He hated the hurt that rose behind her green eyes, but her voice was tight and angry. "We're here because you *agreed to come*. You said we could make a retreat. Get away from the world for a bit. How many times are we going to have this argument?"

"Do you even understand how hard it was for me to take time off?" The words were still coming, like a dam had been breached and was crumbling under the weight behind it. "I haven't published a paper in *two years*. Dr. Stevens said… if I don't publish before the year is out, he's going to replace me, Amy."

"What?" Amy's expression morphed into shock. "You could lose your job?"

"Yeah." Elijah stared down at his hands gripping the water bottle tightly. "Do you have any idea how much this trip is costing us? What if things really do start to fall apart around us? We put thousands of dollars into this trip—a big chunk of our savings is gone, and for what possible benefit?"

Amy's face settled into taut lines, pale beneath her freckles. "For us. Our marriage. What's that worth to you?" She scooted back a bit, crossing her arms over her chest in a self-protective gesture that made Elijah ache as she continued. "We have a baby on the way. Do you want to be a part of your child's life? Because there are times I'm really starting to wonder if you do."

His heart started to pound, defensive anger flaring. "*Every single time*, you have to bring up the baby. Nice." He swallowed hard. "Yes, we have a child on the way. I think you're the one who forgets that, not me. If you were really concerned about this child, you wouldn't have dragged us halfway across the globe to the middle of nowhere in a Third World country! What if something goes wrong? And your practice? You're abandoning it for god knows how long."

"Don't bring up my job, Elijah. My partners have things well under control. Besides, *I'm not the one about to get fired.*"

Amy's brow was furrowed, her chest heaving with her attempts to maintain control of her temper. Elijah knew that look, and right now, he didn't care. No matter what he did, it would never be good enough. Whatever choice he made, it was always the wrong one.

"Why can't I be enough for you, Amy?" Elijah asked, his voice flat. "I gave up my career ambitions to spend more time with you, only for you to disappear into your charity work. I mean, helping strangers is great and all, but it sure as hell shows where your priorities lie. Namely, *not with me*. And now here we are, hanging out at the Saqqara Woodstock festival with a pair of fiddles while Rome burns around us. God, I'm such an *idiot*."

His voice had risen as he spoke. He ran a hand over his face, only to find that he was shaking. Amy had already opened her mouth to say something angry or hurt or both, but the words seemed to lodge in her lungs as she looked past him. Elijah followed her gaze, and found that the woman from the happy hippie trio was approaching them with clear intent. She plopped down a couple of feet away without invitation, sitting with her legs crossed and her arms resting on her knees.

Elijah stared at her, struck as mute as Amy had been — hit by a combination of anger at having been interrupted and embarrassment at being caught having a private argument in a public place.

"Hi, I don't think we've met," said the young woman, whose tanned, faintly boyish features were topped with an unruly mass of brown hair. "I'm Shay. Is everything okay over here?"

Amy and Elijah flickered a glance at each other, embarrassment gaining the upper hand over ire.

"Um… yeah," Amy said, red rising to her pale cheeks. "Sorry. Just a bit of a private disagreement."

"Sure, I get it," Shay said, no judgment in her tone. "It's just that you guys were getting kinda loud. Lots of people here sleep during the day, to escape the heat and because most of the interesting stuff happens at night. We try not to disturb the informal siesta time if we can avoid it. Know what I mean?"

Elijah scrubbed a hand over his scalp, berating himself for needing etiquette lessons from a college kid. "You're absolutely right to say something to us. This was my fault, and I apologize."

Shay smiled. "No need for apologies. I just thought you two might want to know about the unofficial nap time."

She rubbed absently at her left forearm. The movement drew Elijah's eye, and he noticed a path of needle tracks on the paler skin near her elbow. Shay followed his gaze, a strange smile tugging at her wide mouth.

"Problem?" she asked, her tone one of amusement.

Elijah realized how rudely he was staring, and immediately tried to backpedal. "Er... sorry, it's none of my business," he muttered.

The smile widened.

"You think I'm a junkie." Shay blinked at him, and made an attempt to pull her expression into something more neutral. "Wow, you really are new here, I guess?"

Elijah glanced at Amy, who clearly shared his confusion, before turning back to face Shay. "Yes... we just got here an hour or so ago. Like I said, though — it's none of our business."

"For fuck's sake, dude," she said, and her tone was almost pitying now. "Did you two do any research *at all* before you came out here? I'm not a user. *I'm a donor.*"

FOUR

Amy stared at Shay, trying to keep up with the conversation despite her jet lag and roiling emotions after Elijah's bombshell about his job. A *donor*? What the hell was that supposed to mean?

"You know… a *blood donor*." Shay was looking at them like she was starting to think they were both mentally deficient. "For the people here who need it more than we do."

Amy blinked, and a connection clicked into place in her overtired brain. At the same instant, a sinking feeling settled in her stomach. There were, broadly speaking, two kinds of reports to be found online about the peace communes popping up around the world—and about this one in particular.

The first type of story came from the news media, which reported factually about the existence and locations of the various groups camping at historical and spiritual sites. These reports were mostly couched in terms that made the places sound like long-term protest rallies, kind of like the Occupy movement that had briefly gained traction when Amy was younger. There were occasional interviews with people staying at the communes, usually short and carefully edited to convey sound bites about standing up for peace and love in a world gone mad with hate.

The second type came from dodgy websites and internet forums. They showed up in the first few pages of search results for things like 'Saqqara commune' and 'world peace protests.' Amy had stumbled across several of those when she'd gotten curious about the mainstream news stories. She'd skimmed them, rolled her eyes, and dismissed them as being the fevered imaginings of a bunch of crazy basement dwellers and fundamentalists.

Those kinds of forums were full of murmurs about cults. Whispers about demonic influence and unholy rituals. About... *blood* rituals. Brainwashing. Powerful figures drawing in unsuspecting, innocent people for their own nefarious purposes. Things that had seemed so at odds with the rational, idealistic people being interviewed on TV that Amy had scoffed and mashed the 'back' button, rolling her eyes at the seedy underbelly of the internet with its endless trolls and conspiracy theories.

Suddenly, they seemed less crazy. Holy crap. Had they been right? Had *Elijah* been right? Had she done something monumentally stupid, and dragged them both into danger? But Manisha seemed so nice... and she'd talked about them checking out the place for a day to decide if they wanted to stay or not—

Amy's mouth opened and closed a couple of times before words came out. "You... take part in *blood rituals*?"

Shay scoffed. "Seriously, lady. I'd hardly call sterile needles and IV bags a *blood ritual*. You're being a bit over-dramatic. Have you been reading the fundie forums online or something? Fire and brimstone, devil-worship, and all that shit? Look. You've only just gotten here. It's pretty clear neither of you have a clue what's going on in Saqqara, and all the other places where people are gathering together to fight the darkness. Maybe you should just chill here until tonight, and then you can see for yourself."

By this point, Elijah had a faintly glazed look on his face, somewhere on the spectrum between *what-the-ever-loving-hell* and *oh-god-please-kill-me-now*.

"Why wait until tonight?" he asked. "Is that when the orgies and the virgin sacrifices kick off?"

And just like that, Amy was pissed at him again.

Shay laughed, bright and clear. "Not hardly, dude. That's when the vamps come out of their catacombs." She wiggled her fingers dramatically.

"Vamps? As in *vampires*?" Amy said faintly, half-convinced Shay was just messing with them now to get back at Elijah for his sarcasm.

The pitying look was back on Shay's face, though. "Vampires… blood donors. You see where I'm going with this?" She shook her head. "Don't worry, hon—it turns out they're actually the good guys. Like I said, just hang out for a few hours until everyone starts waking up. Don't take my word for it."

With a final cheery smile, Shay scrambled to her feet and turned her back on them, heading away toward the two men she'd been talking and laughing with earlier. Covering a wince at what she expected to see on Elijah's face, Amy turned to look at him. He didn't look angry, though—just tired.

"I know. I *know*," he said. "I gave you my word, and I'll keep it… within certain limitations. We'll stay until the floorshow kicks off tonight and you can see from yourself that this whole thing is a farce. Unless there's some indication that we're in danger—then we're out of here. No debate, Ames. It's not just you and me anymore."

With that, he placed a hand over her stomach, fingers splayed protectively. Tears pricked at the back of Amy's eyes, and she cursed the pregnancy hormones playing merry hell with her emotions and moods.

"All right," she whispered. "If it's all a trick, or if anything alarming happens, we'll leave right away."

-o-o-o-

Far below the milling humans in the compound, the vampire Menkhef sat silently in the chamber where Eris and Trynn slept. He regarded the entwined lovers over hands laced meditatively beneath his chin, keeping watch over more than just his two friends. The catacombs of the South Tomb were still much the same as they had been over the course of the three millennia he'd been buried here. Yet there *were* differences—and not just the ones wrought by the passage of time.

Many of the rooms and corridors still boasted the intricate artwork carved and painted by artists whose bones had long ago crumbled and turned to dust. Now, though, artificial lighting powered by the energy of the unforgiving desert sun illuminated the Stygian tunnels, revealing brilliant colors that still clung to the stone in many places. Even mortal eyes would be able to appreciate every fine line and elegant detail in the corridors and tombs, lit as they were by glowing yellow bulbs.

Human archaeologists had returned to this house of lost souls over the past few decades, clearing away both its resting bones and the ravages of time. They had restored it, in many ways, both aboveground and below. Now, his fellow vampires had gone further, altering Saqqara's very nature by changing it from a necropolis for the dead to an acropolis for the living—a haven for those who clung to the Light in the face of approaching Darkness. In addition to electricity, Xander and the others had also brought in medical equipment for the sterile removal of blood from willing human donors, mattresses for sleeping, and chairs for sitting… including the chair he himself now graced.

The tomb that had once imprisoned him now offered respite from the sun's killing rays. It had become both a refuge and a stronghold.

Menkhef had chosen, without much thought, to claim for himself the same room in which the Pharaoh Qahedjet had once buried his mummified, comatose body. Perhaps that had been a mistake. Certainly, he often seemed to find excuses to be elsewhere, as he had done this day.

Eris and his mate Trynn had wisely decided to claim one of the larger galleries as a sleeping place—one centrally located among the maze of passages snaking beneath the esplanade dominated by the Step Pyramid of Djoser. Menkhef himself did not sleep... had not slept in longer than he could remember. Instead, he cast his mind outward throughout the walled complex, standing watch against the dark forces gathering around them while also blanketing the area with an atmosphere of serenity that the humans would find calming.

It was because of this mental openness that he had become aware of Eris' disturbed slumber, some hours ago. He knew well that—even weeks after the fact—his oldest surviving friend was still rattled by Menkhef's apparent surrender to the demon Bael and his deathlike condition when the others had finally found him. Eris had drained himself to dangerous levels in his determination to revive Menkhef over the course of days rather than decades.

His friend's gamble had paid off, restoring Menkhef to levels of power and vitality he had never before experienced. It was still vaguely discomfiting to catch glimpses of himself in a reflective surface and see the form he'd held on the day Bael had turned him, rather than the wizened and skeletal creature he'd become for so long afterward.

Nonetheless, Menkhef regretted the toll that the past weeks had taken on those he held dear. Perhaps coming here to reassure Eris with his presence through the bond as he slept had merely been selfishness masquerading as compassion... but at least Eris and his mate slumbered more peacefully this way.

Watching them curled together in such quiet contentment was piercingly bittersweet, and despite Menkhef's recent rejuvenation, he found himself feeling tired beyond measure. But none of the others were powerful enough to blanket so many worried humans with an aura of serenity… and how would Menkhef seek out sleep after so long forgoing it, anyway? He wouldn't even know where to start.

Besides, the point was moot; there was far too much to do right now. New humans were arriving almost every day, and with them, new swirls of conflict and fear. Some of them left soon after they arrived, unable to face the truth, while others stayed. Xander and Manisha watched over the aboveground part of the complex by day, but Menkhef and the others made a point of ascending to greet the newcomers once the sun went down each evening.

As it was going down now. After a final few seconds spent in quiet contemplation of Trynn and Eris, Menkhef rose and left the room. Outside, he focused his attention on the bond he shared with the others and sent a mental wake-up call along it, before preparing to ascend from the tunnels to the dry sands and the waiting humans above.

FIVE

Elijah sat propped against the cool stone of one of the faux buildings that made up Heb Sed Court at the southeast edge of Djoser's pyramid, his arm curled around Amy's sleeping form at his side. The ancient Egyptians had built an entire city in miniature inside this complex, but since it was meant for the dead, the houses and monuments weren't real. There were no rooms inside the structures—they were solid stone throughout.

In the world of the dead, appearances suffice, one of the older Egyptologists had quipped when Elijah had been here on a dig a few years ago. It was true enough. Corpses had no use for real buildings—not when fake ones were enough to drive home their wealth and power to the awestruck peasants they'd left behind.

Amy's breath puffed warm and wet against his collarbone. He settled her more comfortably against him as he watched the shadows lengthening into evening. Tired and jet-lagged, she had fallen asleep despite the tension between them... despite their disturbing conversation with the young woman, Shay.

Elijah had become a pathetic enough figure these days that he wasn't above soaking up this unexpected tender interlude. Moments like this didn't come around much for them lately. Amy was always busy with work or some charitable event she'd been hosting or organizing, while Elijah taught his classes. He'd even started teaching some at night once Amy's schedule grew so full that she never seemed to be home anyway.

The truth was, Elijah missed his wife. He had the feeling that a lot of his depression was due to the distance growing ever wider between them. He hoped she wasn't purposely using her career and all the charity work she did outside her practice as an excuse to stay away from him, but after so long, he was really beginning to wonder.

Her work was important to her, though, and his life was humiliating enough without him constantly sniping at her for daring to try and make the world a better place for others. Especially for those less fortunate than they were. So, he endured the lonely nights and the lonely weekends, telling himself he was being selfish and shallow for resenting her absence. If he repeated it to himself often enough, maybe it would eventually start to stick, right?

Elijah wondered if this trip was Amy's way of trying to make things up to him, ill conceived though the idea might have been. She probably thought bringing him back here, to a place with so many fond memories, would have some kind of positive impact on him. So far, it hadn't. Not really. Sure, he'd enjoyed digging up historical artifacts and helping restore the step pyramid from the ravages of time when he'd been here before. Back then, it had been fascinating work—but none of that mattered now.

What did matter at this very moment, was that his wife—the beautiful, intelligent woman he still loved more than life itself—was here, lying trustingly in his arms, setting all of her worries aside for a few fleeting hours of rest. He didn't want to waste a second of it. He'd hold her like this for as long as she'd allow it.

After another hour or so, the strange new world inside Saqqara's necropolis began to stir. The sun was setting, and scents of something cooking outside stirred Elijah's hunger, eliciting a rumble loud enough to wake the dead from their underground tombs.

The dead, and also his wife.

Amy's eyes fluttered open, and she glanced up at Elijah, whose left arm was still wrapped around her waist.

"Hey," he said, offering her a tentative smile. "Did you sleep well?"

The answering drowsy curve of her lips lacked the wariness it might have had if she'd been fully awake. The sight of it warmed him more than the beating sun had managed earlier. Why could they never seem to hold onto these fleeting moments where everything became simple again?

"Very well, especially under the circumstances," she replied in a sleepy rasp. "What time is it?"

Elijah tugged his phone out of his pocket with his free hand, but it had died. He wondered with a pang of uneasiness if he'd be able to charge it here. He'd have to ask someone. "I'm not sure—my battery's dead. I'll have to dig out my watch. The sun's going down, though. You hungry?"

"Starving." She rolled up enough to kiss him, and the look of almost painful affection on her face was one he'd missed desperately. She didn't say anything further because she didn't have to. Neither did he. If they started talking about anything of substance, they would probably ruin things again by fighting, and he wasn't ready for that yet.

Instead, he leaned down and pressed another brief kiss to her chapped lips. "Something smells good. Probably not gourmet fare, but definitely good enough to eat. Let's go see about feeding that baby of ours."

Elijah rose to his feet as Amy sat up the rest of the way, yawning and stretching her arms. The movement showed off the toned lines of her body beneath her loose cotton shirt. She peered up at him with the sweetest smile on her face as she caught him looking. And for one fleeting moment, Elijah believed—irrationally—that everything was going to be okay.

"Come on, Ames. Let's see what passes for dinner in the desert." He winked, holding out his hand to her.

She accepted it, allowing him to help her to her feet, and then her nose wrinkled.

"Oh my god, I need to pee." She snorted, settling one hand over her belly. "Damned hormones. I'm barely even showing! How bad is this going to be five months from now?"

Something hit Elijah in the gut as he pictured her heavy with their child. It was part panic, part longing, and part... something else. He covered it quickly.

"Bad enough that I'm glad I'm a man, for sure," he said lightly. "Come on, let's find you a portaloo." He took her hand and they ventured out of their tent, heading through the compound toward the makeshift lavatories Manisha had pointed out to them when they arrived.

After they were done using the facilities and washing up, they met up again and followed the scent of cooking food to a huge red and white striped tent. Outside it, a line was already forming. Elijah and Amy stood amongst other visitors waiting their turn for food.

Under a canopy near the back, three people were manning propane cook stoves, covered with various large pots billowing steam into the dry, greedy air. The scent of spices and herbs was tantalizing. While standing in line, Elijah dug discreetly into his wallet. Despite the rules against stealing, there was no way to know what kind of people might be paying attention to the resources they had brought with them. He felt as though he should be more worried than he actually was. Despite the air of calm serenity around them, there was no point in flashing cash around.

Amy's gaze wandered over their surroundings, analyzing everything—the people, the tents, the way things were set up. Elijah followed her gaze, beginning to wonder with real interest who was behind this setup. Somebody had invested a hell of a lot of time and money into it, and people generally didn't do that unless they planned to get something tangible out of their investment.

"How much do you think the food costs?" he asked, trying to start a conversation that wouldn't devolve into sniping. Maybe keeping things light was the best course of action. They'd had a nice afternoon despite the disturbing conversation with Shay earlier. Why rock the boat?

Amy shrugged. "No idea. If it's too high, maybe we can hike into the village tomorrow morning and pick up supplies there."

The line moved up two more paces, and an older woman standing in front of them turned to look at them. "The food is free here. It costs nothing for guests of the compound."

Elijah blinked at her. "Seriously?"

She tilted her head, as though surprised by his disbelieving tone. "Yes."

The woman's face was deeply wrinkled and tanned by the sun. She had clearly been here a while. She wore sandals and light clothing in the Egyptian style. Thick, grey streaks highlighted her brown hair.

She seemed happy. Easy inside her skin.

"How do they pay for all this?" Elijah asked. Surely he couldn't be the only person suspicious of this place. After all, any intelligent person knew that nothing came free. And judging by the resources around them – solar panels, expensive tents, food and water – someone was paying through the nose for this operation. It couldn't possibly be for no personal gain.

"I'm not certain. But nobody pays here—not for anything." The woman continued. "Though the organizers do encourage long-term visitors to volunteer their time and help keep everything running smoothly."

Elijah tried to keep his expression neutral, even though his bullshit detector was tingling at full-strength now. This couldn't be what it appeared. Nothing so seemingly altruistic ever was.

Stop, Elijah admonished himself. He'd promised Amy they would stay at least until the show later, to find out for themselves what was really going on here. And honestly, he couldn't deny a growing sense of curiosity now, especially regarding Shay's story of the mysterious figures at the center of this gathering. If they were the ones funding this thing, what was their angle?

Because it sure as hell wasn't blood farming for vampires. No way. Would they all be like that Manisha woman who had greeted them when they arrived? Unassuming and normal? And if they were—if nothing alarming happened—what then? Elijah's sixth sense had been urging him that this trip was bad news since they'd arrived, but now he was getting sucked into it, wanting to play amateur detective and figure out what was going on.

Maybe that's how they get you, his paranoia offered helpfully.

"Manisha said they use recycled graywater to grow vegetables here," Amy mused, still looking around with obvious fascination. "I'd like to see what they're doing with the gardens."

As Amy and Elijah waited in the line for food, volunteers standing at a long table were spooning scoopfuls of rice, beans, and cooked vegetables onto plates. They accepted a pair of generous servings once they reached the front of the queue, and Amy politely thanked the server. A kindly old man at the end of the table smiled, handing them each a cold bottle of water along with some napkins and utensils to eat with.

Outside the tent, the level of conversation and ambient noise grew noticeably. Something was happening.

"Sounds like the show is about to start." Elijah tipped his chin to a small area of seating set in front of the food tent. "Let's find a place to sit before the commotion gets out of hand."

The noise echoing among the archaic stone structures rose to a surprising din. Most of the people sitting at the nearby tables abandoned their meals and rose to their feet, craning to look toward the center of the esplanade.

As he and Amy moved to set their plates down, a ragged cheer rose around them. Amy gasped, and his attention flew to her. She was staring not at the crowd, but above it, her mouth forming into a round *oh* of surprise.

"What is it?" Elijah asked, trying to follow her gaze to whatever had caught her attention.

"Elijah… have you ever seen anything like that in your life?" Her voice held a note of pure amazement, and her eyes were wide as her hand closed around his upper arm, holding tight.

Then he saw them. Beautiful owls were circling the esplanade overhead—at least half a dozen, maybe more.

Owls.

Several different species.

In the middle of the desert.

That was definitely not something he'd ever seen before while staying here. Sure, there were owls in Egypt, but he'd never witnessed so many different kinds in one small area. Wild animals should have wanted nothing to do with an excited crowd of humans in a confined area. And they would never behave as though they were putting on an intricate aerial ballet for the onlookers. Had the people here been... feeding them, or something?

As he watched with the same stunned fascination as Amy, the avian predators took turns swooping down amongst the crowd in a manner that seemed almost... *playful.* He and Amy stood staring at the sky, their food forgotten on the table next to them. Eventually, the owls disappeared one by one, diving too low to be seen over the sea of heads, and not returning

Elijah narrowed his eyes, searching the skies for the missing birds.

"Okay. That was... weird." He scratched his chin.

The crowd's open glee subsided into quiet murmuring now that the show appeared to be over. Elijah started to turn to Amy, but a swirl of cool breeze broke through the sudden stillness. His gaze fell on a curling cloud of thick, white vapor as it rolled into an open area a few yards away from where they were standing. Any words he might have been about to say died in his throat.

Amy tightened her grip on Elijah's arm and moved closer to him, tension coiling her muscles. "What the hell is that?"

He glanced down at her pale features, but her eyes went wide and she pointed toward the center of the mist. *Fog machine*, he started to say, only to have his breath catch in his chest as the vapor appeared to pull into itself, condensing into solidity in a way that just didn't happen in nature.

The solidifying form stepped forward, taking on human shape even as swirls of mist trailed behind it, like it was being poured into existence from the thin desert air. Elijah nearly stumbled back a step as he attempted to convince himself this wasn't real. Things like this didn't happen outside of movie special effects. This was just an illusion orchestrated to pull them further into… whatever this crazy place turned out to be.

The last wisps of vapor disappeared into the now very solid form of a man. He looked… real. Undeniably real and present—confirmed when several people in the crowd hurried forward and touched him.

The figure stood like a statue of some ancient pharaoh, brought to life by the energy of the people surrounding him. His chiseled features, straight nose and high cheekbones were pure Egyptian royalty—the real deal, right down to the kilt-like linen *shendyt* belted neatly around his waist.

Next to Elijah, Amy stared shamelessly as though unable to look away from the man's dark eyes and full lips. Of course, as soon as Elijah followed her gaze, he was caught again as well, that pit inside his stomach which had opened the moment they'd touched down in Cairo growing ever deeper.

Grab Amy and run, or your lives will never be the same again, said a voice inside him.

And yet, his feet remained rooted to the sand, his eyes glued to the figure that had materialized from thin air in the middle of the crowded concourse. The people surrounding the man weren't mobbing him, exactly, but they were certainly eager to be close, like he was some kind of god to be worshipped.

"This is… unreal." Amy stared at the scene in awe, sheer wonderment in her demeanor. "Tell me you're seeing the same thing I'm seeing…"

A searching glance at her face showed that Amy had definitely drunk the Kool-Aid, and Elijah had to suppress a shiver despite the heat. He returned his attention to the man greeting the people around him, clasping shoulders, laying a hand on their backs briefly in greeting before moving on to others.

Obviously, Amy wasn't the only one around here who liked the taste of Kool-Aid. Holy shit.

The mystery man's expression was calm—unruffled and cool as he made his rounds through the crowd. He nodded occasionally but did not speak, though the people approaching him frequently spoke to him.

And… now he was coming straight toward Elijah and Amy.

Caught between several conflicting impulses, Elijah made an abortive move to place himself between Amy and the enigmatic figure. His feet were glued in place, though. His gaze, trapped by eyes which had looked nearly black before, but now kindled with an inner glow the color of molten bronze. Impossibly, a deep voice rolled through Elijah's mind even though the man's lips hadn't moved.

Do not fear. You are both welcome in the stronghold of Saqqara.

Again, Elijah felt that he should move or protest as the man lifted an elegant, long-fingered hand to brush a lock of hair back from Amy's face with a gossamer touch... but the moment was already past. Then, the same hand closed fleetingly over the junction of Elijah's neck and shoulder, surprisingly cool where it brushed his skin.

Now, more than ever, we must hold fast to the things that are important, continued the silent voice. *Do not allow the Darkness to steal away your Light.*

A look of wistfulness flickered across that carved-stone face as he looked between the two of them.

"What—" Elijah began hoarsely, but the man had already moved onto the next knot of people, leaving him and Amy gaping at a broad, well-muscled back.

SIX

Amy stared unblinkingly at the receding figure who had just spoken directly to her soul without uttering a single word aloud. He might as well have run a blade through her heart and left her bleeding out on the sand—all of the things she possessed and all of the things she lacked pouring into a messy red puddle at her feet.

She realized she'd been holding her breath and gasped sharply for air, her chest burning. The ragged sound drew Elijah's attention, breaking him free from his earlier paralysis. His handsome, dark-skinned face blurred oddly in her vision, like she was looking at him through a window lashed by rain. Callused palms cupped her face.

"Ames, you're crying." He sounded struck, like the same invisible knife had slipped between his ribs, too. "What is it?"

"He's right," she said, everything suddenly becoming clear even as her vision continued to blur with saltwater. "Oh god, Elijah... he's right. What have we been doing to each other?"

Elijah shuddered, though his hands remained gentle on her face, like someone holding delicate glass.

"I love you, Amy. Still. Forever and always, I never want to lose you, or god forbid, give you up.

Ever." His voice was hoarse. "You have to know that, don't you?"

"*Elijah.*" Amy swallowed hard, and tried to blink her eyes clear enough to see his expression properly.

He leaned down, pulling her into his arms, holding her tightly to his chest as he used to do so long ago… like he could shelter her from the whole world with his body. "We need to find someplace quiet to talk, sweetheart."

"Okay. Bring the plates," she added as her stomach rumbled, reminding her of her baby's need for food.

Elijah chuckled, though it sounded a bit watery. "Of course." He grabbed their plates and led Amy through the esplanade toward their tent, searching for a quiet place where they could finally clear the air, years after they should have done.

It was telling that Elijah hadn't said a word about the impossible nature of what they'd just seen and experienced. Amy might not have been the hard-core skeptic that Elijah was, but she knew the moment she really stopped and thought about the last few minutes, she would have to make some serious decisions about what was and wasn't part of her worldview. Right now, though, talking about their future—and their past—was more important to her.

She was a bit surprised that it seemed to be more important to her husband, too.

He led her past groups of people clustered around musicians, and others who seemed to be listening to storytellers. There were kids here, she realized with a jolt. People had uprooted their whole families to come to the middle of the desert and do... what? Were they hiding from the darkness, or confronting it?

Elijah led her away from the crowds to a corner of the walled complex that was nearly untouched by the electric lighting—a ledge beside a staircase that led down to one of the lower chambers of the tombs.

"Here." Elijah sat along the ledge and patted the masonry beside him. "Let's sit here."

Amy sat beside him, her eyes still damp.

He stroked her face again. "Please, eat. We'll talk right afterward."

She nodded, taking a few moments to eat the vegetables and rice on her plate, then downing her bottle of water. She took a napkin, dabbing at the salty tear trails on her cheeks. Then she leaned back, letting her gaze roam upward.

"Wow, would you look at those stars," she breathed. The dark desert sky was awash with millions of pinpricks, the Milky Way clearly visible as a streak above their heads. "It really is beautiful here. I can see why you loved coming. I wish I understood why you stopped traveling to digs."

The air was cooling rapidly now that the sun was down. Amy ran her hands over her upper arms in an absent rhythm, staying silent while Elijah struggled to organize his thoughts.

"You were gone a lot," he said eventually, "working after hours. I thought if I gave up my research, you'd stay home more." Elijah scrubbed at his chin. "It was stupid. I see that now. We'd started growing apart long before then. But when I was gone on digs all the time, you found ways to cope. It's my fault, really. You got involved in your charities because I abandoned you, but by the time I came back, it was too late. You'd already pulled away."

Amy sat beside him, quietly contemplating his words.

This conversation had been a long time coming. They'd both been lazy with their marriage. She knew she was lucky he still cared enough to even want to save it. If it weren't for the baby, she thought he might very well have left her already. Fate had given them a second chance to fix things, and she was determined to make it count.

"You're not to blame," Amy said, laying her hand over Elijah's on the warm stone ledge. "We both are. I complained a lot when you traveled. I didn't appreciate how dependent your career was on it."

He snorted. "Only because I never explained it to you properly. I told myself I didn't want to worry you, but it was more a case of not wanting to face the choices I was making. Being a college professor is tough these days, but it's not the only thing I can do, Ames. I could always go back and teach high school again."

She frowned. "No, Elijah. You love university teaching. I would never ask that of you."

"You don't have to ask." He set his hands on her belly. "I'd do it for us. For our family. Whatever the answer is, we'll figure it out together."

She covered his hands with hers, knowing that in a few short months, he would be able to feel the baby move when they did this.

"Thank you for bringing me here," he continued. "That man, whoever… whatever he was… he was right." Elijah swallowed. "And so are you."

Another tear overflowed. It ran down Amy's cheek as Elijah reached up, wiping it away with the base of his thumb.

"Don't cry, baby. Please, just listen. I got depressed, that's all. And if I'm being honest, maybe a little jealous. It felt like you were moving on without me."

Amy swallowed the lump that was forming in her throat. "I never meant for that to happen. This is my fault, too."

"I'm not trying to place blame. When I gave up research, I think I expected you to give up your charities. But that was completely selfish of me. I was wrong." He pushed a curl of red hair off Amy's shoulder. "I know why you did it. Truth is, I felt it too. Something important was missing in our marriage. It still is, to be honest. I'm not naive, I know this trip can't be a cure-all, and I have no clue what will fix things for good. What I do know is that I'm still completely, *crazy* in love with you. I'm committed to our marriage, no matter what." He held her cheeks, gazing deeply into her eyes. "Our family is worth fighting for."

Amy made a small noise in her throat and surged forward, kissing her husband deeply before pulling back enough to rest their foreheads together. "I love you, Elijah. I don't know how to fix things either, but please—never doubt how much I love you."

He nodded, and she felt the pull of the small motion against her skin where he still pressed against her.

"Come on," he said, pulling back a little. "Let's go back now. You look exhausted, and I know I am."

He took her hand and led the way back to their tent, dropping off their dishes and cutlery at the mess tent on the way. Once there, they shuffled inside and closed themselves off from the rest of Saqqara, zipping the door shut. Amy curled up in Elijah's arms, feeling a tiny flame of hope that this would be the first step of many toward a better future. It wasn't the solution, and there was certainly more work to be done, but maybe the conversation they'd just had marked a new beginning for their family.

"I do love you Amy," Elijah said as he settled her into his embrace. "I'd give anything to have all the answers, but I don't. All I can do is promise that I'll be right here beside you for as long as you'll have me."

"That's forever, Elijah," Amy whispered. "Now sleep. Whatever else is missing in our lives, you and this baby are my family, and I *will not* let us fail. That much, I swear."

The arms around her tightened, and Amy squeezed back just as hard.

SEVEN

"I'm not sure I've ever seen you this distracted during a game before, my friend," Eris said. "And after more than sixteen hundred years, that's saying something."

Menkhef dragged his attention back to the marble chessboard, realizing with some surprise that his king was in check. Across the room, Trynn looked up from her book, raising an eyebrow as she straightened from her sideways slouch in the chair.

"Don't tell me you're going to beat him?" she asked, sounding intrigued.

Eris snorted. Menkhef narrowed his eyes at her—a quelling expression. He quickly moved a castle to remove the check, casting an eye over the remaining pieces to reassess the state of the game as Eris moved his knight in reply.

"I doubt there's much danger of that," Eris said in a dry tone.

"Well, you shouldn't have tipped him off to what was happening," Trynn observed with some asperity. "What the hell kind of strategy is that?"

Eris' wash of amusement across the mental connection was a balm. "Probably a poor one. But I'm more interested in the reason for his woolgathering than I am in the fleeting satisfaction of a stolen win. Aren't you?"

"Hmm. Fair point." Trynn's sharp eyes pinned Menkhef. "So, spill. What's got your knickers in a twist this morning, Snag? I thought things had been going pretty well the last few days."

It was a reasonable question, even when couched in such flippant terms. There was no reason his thoughts should keep returning to the unhappy human couple who'd arrived the previous day, seeking answers to all the wrong questions in this faraway place. Though it was out of character for him, he allowed his impressions of the pair to leak out through the bond—from their desperate love to their desperate unhappiness, and their understandable fear for the tiny new life they nurtured against the backdrop of an uncertain future.

Trynn stared at him in surprise after the unaccustomed outpouring, her book lying forgotten against her knees. Pages slipped past the restraining finger she'd laid over the edges, losing her place. Abruptly, she came to her senses and stopped the cascade of paper, blinking at him across the length of the room.

"Thinking of getting into the marriage counseling game?" she asked, clearly taken aback by the strength of his reaction to the unlikely couple. "No offense, but I'm not sure it really suits you."

Unsurprisingly, Eris was watching him with a more insightful expression, absently twirling a white pawn he'd taken earlier back and forth between his fingers. He cocked his head. "You're a tight-lipped bastard, my old friend, but I hear the things you don't say as well as the things you do.

Be patient for a little while longer, and I'm certain what you lost will be returned to you, just as it was returned to the rest of us."

Menkhef arched an eyebrow, his face giving away nothing as he slid his bishop diagonally across the board. *Mate in seven,* he sent, effectively closing the conversation before it could turn to things he wasn't ready to discuss, even with people he cherished as much as he cherished these two.

-o-o-o-

Despite his exhaustion, Elijah spent a long time staring into the darkness inside the tent. Amy had once again fallen asleep almost immediately, only the occasional small noise or movement as she dreamed marring the stillness of her body. He spent the time thinking, retreading familiar territory regarding their marriage troubles without reaching any new conclusions.

It was a relief beyond measure to have things out in the open—to know that Amy wanted to work things out as much as he did. Maybe he shouldn't have doubted that in the first place, but one thing he'd learned the hard way over the past few years was that depression could whisper all sorts of lies into your ear and make them sound perfectly believable. Now, though, relieved or not, he wasn't willing to sit by while the two of them slid right back into the quicksand.

There had to be an answer.

But what, exactly, was the question? They'd both used language about feeling like something was missing in their lives. Elijah frequently found himself thinking that he wasn't enough for Amy. Something inside him was convinced that no matter what he did, it would never fill the gap. Whether he was a career-driven badass or a stay-at-home domestic dad, he didn't think he'd ever be able to erase that searching, faraway look from her eyes—the look that said, 'I need something more.'

After their talk, he was starting to understand that her seeming desperation to fill every moment of every day with activity was her way of trying to deal with whatever need she had that he wasn't meeting. Or maybe it wasn't to do with him at all? Turning his focus toward his own unmet needs was surprisingly uncomfortable. He made himself do it anyway.

It was far too easy to fall into the trap of thinking he was only unhappy because Amy was unhappy and becoming ever more emotionally distant toward him. Was that the whole truth, though? If she woke up in the morning to become the perfect, emotionally attentive wife... if she gave up her charities and focused on their relationship... would he magically become a happy and fulfilled person?

No, he thought with brutal honesty. No, he wouldn't. The answer was obvious when he stripped away all the bullshit and really thought about it, because he had never in his damned life been a happy and fulfilled person.

He had experienced moments of happiness. He had experienced moments of fulfillment. But from adolescence onward he'd always yearned for something both unreachable and indefinable. Something... *missing*.

And so he'd come full circle.

There was no question that Amy had filled an empty place inside him. From what she'd said tonight, he'd filled an empty place inside her, too. But their rough edges rubbed up against each other, grating together rather than sliding into place like puzzle pieces. In many ways they were too alike. In others, so different that they often seemed to have nothing in common.

A few months ago, before Amy got pregnant, Elijah had been convinced that she was about to leave him. He started having dreams of seeing her in another man's arms—hazy images that haunted him even after he woke up. The biggest problem was, it wasn't necessarily jealousy that tortured him afterward. For weeks, he obsessed over the dreams, indulging in several clandestine internet searches he really wasn't proud of before coming to the conclusion that he had an unwanted and extremely humiliating cuckolding fetish.

In what was probably their ugliest marital fight to date, he'd snapped, "Well maybe we should have an open marriage and start seeing other people!" in response to something she'd said that had pissed him off.

Good god, he couldn't even remember now what the argument had originally been about. How utterly ridiculous.

Not that it mattered—he might as well have slapped Amy across the cheek, from her reaction. She'd physically staggered back a step, the blood draining from her face until it was chalky.

"You... want to see other women?" she'd whispered hoarsely.

Frustration had kept the words coming despite the warning signs. "I thought you might want to see other men, since I'm obviously not good enough for you!"

The blood that had left her cheeks returned to color them bright red, and her eyes snapped fire as she'd hissed, "If you want to get rid of me so badly, hire a fucking lawyer and serve me with divorce papers, damn it! I won't be your castoff leftovers!"

It was the first time either of them had used the 'D' word, and the pain lurking behind Amy's anger ensured that Elijah never brought up the idea of alternative lifestyles again. Not long afterward, they'd hit a slight thaw, and fate combined with faulty birth control brought a new twist into their lives. Elijah was damned if he'd rock the boat—not when that boat now held a child with Amy's bright green eyes and his tight curls... or whatever other combination of traits their genetics happened to produce.

The noises of happy people outside were starting to fade when fatigue finally began to pull him down toward sleep. He fought it, knowing that he still had no good answers, no fresh ideas. He dreaded the thought of slipping straight back into the mess they'd been wallowing in for the past couple of years.

They needed a fresh perspective. They needed... *they... needed...*

Elijah's eyes slipped closed, the stuffy confines of the tent giving way to an arid landscape of dreams.

EIGHT

The sun was disappearing behind the swaying palm trees on the western bank of the Nile when Heqab returned from an afternoon spent training new archers to shoot from the back of a chariot. Several people greeted him as he approached the edge of the village, but he restricted himself to brusque nods in return.

Passersby would see only the Captain of the Guard, hurrying from the training grounds to his evening duties in the royal household. And that was exactly what he wished them to see. They did not need to know precisely what those duties entailed—or, more to the point, they did not need to know that it wasn't duty hurrying his feet toward the palace, but desire.

As was usual in the weeks since Heqab's oldest friend had extended him a shockingly unusual offer, the palace was deserted when he arrived. The scribes, servants, and supplicants had all been sent away with the setting sun, leaving the building quiet and peaceful as golden light slanted through the reed coverings hanging across the western windows. It was hot inside the stone structure. The red blocks were slow to absorb the sun's rays in the morning, but they were also slow to give up the baking heat they had absorbed once evening came.

Heqab moved through the sparsely furnished rooms until he reached the open courtyard at the building's center. There, an artful arrangement of ferns and small trees gave the illusion of a secluded glade, the greenery combining with the fresh air to make the surroundings feel noticeably cooler. He stopped at the entrance, resting a hand on the sandstone pillar next to him to steady himself as the now familiar feeling of this being a dream washed over him.

A divan with polished legs carved in the forms of lions sat in the shade of a date palm at the far end of the courtyard. It was not the fine workmanship of the low couch that held Heqab's gaze, however. It was the people resting on the cushions. The nomarch—ruler of the local principality and Heqab's dear friend since childhood—reclined on the divan with his queen resting against his chest as he hand-fed her figs. His dark eyes held nothing of their usual penetrating ruthlessness; instead, he watched his wife with such depths of affection that Heqab caught his breath.

The small sound must have reached the pair, because Nebetta's gaze flickered to him and held. She very deliberately swallowed the morsel of fruit she'd just nibbled from her husband's fingers, and a smile graced her luscious lips.

She was stunning, with large, brown eyes, long black hair plaited into dozens of tiny braids, and sumptuous curves. Her regal bearing hid a mischievous twinkle that very few people got to see, and she employed it now, stretching in her husband's arms until the loose linen *kalasiris* she wore slid lower on her torso, baring one breast to his hungry eyes. Then she winked at him.

Her husband lifted a winged brow and followed her gaze to where Heqab was standing. A touch of a teasing smile curved one corner of his full mouth.

"Good evening, Guard Captain." His voice was deep and commanding, though the overly formal greeting carried the same hint of fond teasing as his expression. "We were starting to think you found the company of your recruits more stimulating than ours."

Heqab wrested himself free of his momentary paralysis. *This was real. They wanted him here – it wasn't a dream.* He affected a lazy grin, examining his ragged fingernails for a moment as though the sight in front of him didn't affect him right down to his marrow.

"*Really*, Your Excellence… if my recruits stimulated me half as much as our queen does, I suspect there would be immediate rioting within the barracks." He made sure to inject a note of tartness into the words, and was rewarded by a rich chuckle in counterpoint with Nebetta's light laughter.

"I suspect you're quite right about that," said the nomarch, his voice still tinged with real amusement.

Nebetta grinned at him as he pushed away from the stone column he'd been leaning against and sauntered toward them. "Politeness dictates I ask how your day was," she said, "but I find myself much more interested in a kiss. Menkhef has been teasing me terribly while we waited."

As though to illustrate, Menkhef cupped Nebetta's naked breast, his thumb tweaking the dusky point of her nipple. She made a low noise and arched like a cat, the movement sending an arrow of lust straight to Heqab's groin.

"My day was fine, my Queen," he managed, his flesh hardening almost painfully beneath his belted linen *shendyt*. "But I suspect it's about to get even better. Remind me to thank our esteemed ruler for his efforts in keeping you… entertained… in my absence."

Nebetta's eyes grew heavy-lidded, and Heqab started shedding clothing and leather armor as he went. His words hadn't been meant as fatuous diplomacy… merely the truth. As he drew near the divan, the smell of Nebetta's arousal tickled his nostrils. He'd learned over the past weeks that his old friend had a penchant for drawn-out love play—one that meshed rather well with Heqab's own tendency for not beating around the bush.

So it was that he had no guilt whatsoever in dropping to his knees, dragging Nebetta toward him until her loose skirt ruched around her thighs, and burying his face in her sex. She'd asked for a kiss, after all. She hadn't specified *where*.

The noise she made was wholly gratifying, though it made the ache in his cock grow almost unbearable.

"Brute," she managed, her tone of accusation not terribly convincing.

He smiled against her flesh, dipping his tongue deeper to taste the pulse of wetness that belied her feigned outrage, making her shudder.

Meanwhile, Menkhef gathered a handful of her dark braids and used the light grip to turn her gaze up to his.

"This is what you get for agreeing to take a soldier as a lover, my beloved," he observed, his voice a rumble of warm decadence. "Soldiers conquer."

He lifted his free hand and rubbed over Nebetta's lower lip with the pad of his thumb. Heqab dragged his tongue up the length of her slit, lapping roughly at the nub of her pleasure. She gasped, letting her husband's thumb slide into her mouth, her soft lips closing around it and her eyes fluttering closed. Heqab groaned against her sensitive flesh at the sight, and the vibration was apparently too much for her—she writhed, her body growing taut between them the instant before her hips jerked, signaling her release.

Watching her, Heqab knew exactly what he wanted this evening. He continued to nuzzle her sex, drawing out her pleasure until she was a limp, shivering mess between them. With a glance at Menkhef, he rose and manhandled her spent body into position so she was kneeling on shaky legs at the edge of the divan, giving him a fine view of her rounded buttocks as she faced her husband.

Menkhef was still sprawled against the divan's backrest, his legs parted, one bare foot resting on the floor. Nebetta attacked the clasp of his belt with unsteady fingers while Heqab slid the loose folds of her linen skirt up to drape over her lower back, baring her to him. She finally defeated the closure of her husband's *shendyt* belt and dragged the fabric out of her way. His prick sprang up, as hard and ready as Heqab's.

Nebetta already looked debauched, and that was *before* she leaned forward, the lips that had closed around her husband's thumb now closing over the head of his cock instead. Heqab couldn't hold back the growl that rumbled up from his chest. His hands closed around Nebetta's hips, fingers gripping tight enough to leave marks. He sheathed himself inside her dripping passage with a single unforgiving slide, not stopping until his sac slapped against her folds.

She cried out around the hard flesh in her mouth, and Menkhef's head fell back, a huff of breath escaping his lungs as his much-vaunted control finally started to slip. It thrilled Heqab anew each night simply to realize that he was wanted here… but it thrilled him even more to know that he could reduce both the nomarch and his queen to the status of writhing, wanton animals.

He pulled back slowly and thrust into Nebetta's welcoming heat again, driving her forward onto her husband's cock. Menkhef gathered her braided hair away from her face with a shaky hand, letting Heqab set their rhythm. For long minutes, only the sounds of flesh on flesh and Nebetta's low moans broke the stillness of the courtyard as the evening darkened around them.

Surprisingly, Menkhef was the first to break, arching in silent release as he spilled his seed down Nebetta's throat. Her choked keening noise and the feeling of her inner muscles clamping around Heqab's cock as she came caused the heat coiling at the base of his spine to explode outward. His vision went white as he spurted his essence as deep inside her as he could get. When he had nothing more to give, he half-collapsed over her back, catching himself with one hand on the edge of the divan to keep his weight off her.

His softening prick slid free of her welcoming depths and they both shuddered. Nebetta sagged into her husband's embrace, while Heqab managed a marginally controlled sideways slide onto the ground, twisting so that his back leaned against the edge of the low couch, even with Menkhef's hip.

A slender, female arm draped around him from behind, soft fingers splaying over the center of his chest where his pounding heartbeat was gradually returning to normal. He let his head fall back on the cushions, eyes closed, soaking in the touch. A smile tugged at his lips as Nebetta's fingers curled in his dark chest hair and tugged playfully.

"After being drowned with so much seed at once," she said, her voice sounding fucked-out and throaty, "I'll be lucky if I don't fall pregnant with twins."

Heqab's smile grew wider, even though he couldn't be bothered to move yet. "You'll birth a pair of godlings, and throw the Pharaoh Qahedjet into palpitations," he murmured.

A larger hand closed over the juncture of Heqab's neck and shoulder, the fingers strong and callused. "If that happens, they will have need of a strong guardsman to watch over them," Menkhef said, his voice rich and soothing. "Fortunately, I know just the man for the job."

NINE

Amy awoke with a familiar form spooned around her back. What had become considerably less familiar over the past couple of months was the morning wood nestled between her ass cheeks as Elijah's warm breath puffed against the back of her neck. Her body reacted before her mind had a chance to catch up, tightening in pleasant anticipation at the prospect of sex after going well over two months without.

For all she knew, the last time they'd made love might well have been the time she unexpectedly got pregnant. Shortly afterward, their brief relationship thaw had chilled again, and a few weeks after that, she'd come down with morning sickness that stubbornly refused to confine itself to the mornings. Later they'd been planning—and fighting about—this trip, and suddenly it had been more than ten weeks since she'd gotten any action.

If that was about to change in the next few minutes, was she really okay with the idea of getting it on inside a flimsy tent surrounded by people in dozens of other flimsy tents? Elijah made a low, male noise in his chest. He flexed his hips, rutting against her from behind, and she decided that, yeah, she kind of *was* okay with it at this point. The arm he'd slung over her waist shifted, his hand closing around her hip and pressing her against his hard length. Her pussy throbbed, getting on board with the program immediately.

Hot damn. Whatever dream he was having, Amy was woman enough to admit that she was jealous as hell right now. Going with the moment, she wriggled her hips, increasing the friction and causing his fingers to tighten over her hipbone. Just as she was trying to figure out the most efficient way to start shedding clothes in such a confined space, Elijah froze, going very, very still behind her.

An instant later, he shuffled back, putting a careful inch of space between them, and her stomach sank in disappointment. Bracing herself for rejection, she rolled onto her back so she could see him.

"Elijah? You… uh… you didn't have to stop on my account…"

The expression on his face halted her in her tracks. He looked… guilty. There was no other word for it. His face had gone positively gray beneath the rich mahogany of his skin. Why would he be guilty about a sex dream? Unless—

Unless he'd been dreaming about another woman. Not *her*. Not the harpy he was married to who constantly fought with him and snapped at him and dragged him halfway across the world when he didn't want to go. Her stomach churned.

His eyes darted around, as though searching for an escape route. "It's…" he started, only to cut himself off and begin again. "There are too many people around, that's all. Someone will hear us."

He's lying, her internal bullshit detector pronounced with certainty.

She tried to laugh off the awkward moment. "Yeah. Um. I guess you're right. Last thing we need is Shay unzipping the tent and sticking her head in to tell us we're being too loud, right?"

His answering smile looked tight and uncomfortable, but relief rolled off him in waves. "Right," he agreed. "We wouldn't want to interrupt people's *siesta time*."

At that, she became aware of the world beyond the stifling atmosphere of tension inside the tent. It was light outside, the bright desert sun illuminating the interior through the fabric and driving the temperature up.

"Geez," Elijah said, scrubbing a hand over his scalp as though to brush away whatever had just happened between them. "We must have slept ten hours straight. We should, uh, go see if they're still serving food. You need to eat regularly."

Amy tried to let the weird interval go. Even if Elijah had dreamed something that would legitimately make him feel guilty, it's not like you could hold someone to account for the random images that popped up in their heads when they slept. God knew, she'd had her share of weird sex dreams over the years, including ones where she was having sex with more than one guy at a time. She'd be a hell of a hypocrite if she went all judgy on her husband for getting some illicit action while he was asleep.

Besides, he was right about all the people who might hear them, and he was right about her needing to eat. She also felt more than a little gross after twenty-four hours in the same clothes, and desperately wanted to clean herself up. The urge to pee rose to join the growing litany of reasons why having sex right now was a bad idea.

Pregnancy was weird—what with the cravings for strange foods, the roller coaster of swirling emotions, and losing control over body functions she'd always taken for granted. On the positive side, her previously underwhelming boobs had grown three cup sizes... maybe someday she'd even get to enjoy that fact.

Amy looked forward to the day she would feel their baby move inside her. All her friends said four months, so hopefully it wouldn't be too much longer. She smiled, rubbing her belly for a moment, saying good morning to her unborn child. A much-needed sense of peace fluttered inside her chest, settling. Even with the momentary strangeness between her and Elijah this morning, after their talk last night the fear of having to raise her child without its father was fading away.

Today would be a fresh start, she decided. For all three of them.

"That was a better night's sleep than I expected considering we're camping in the desert," she said, forcing positivity into her tone. "Though I may have to make a run for the portaloos before I tackle breakfast. Coming?"

"Yep," Elijah confirmed, easing through the tent flap and reaching his hand out for hers. She took it and he helped her out of the tent, zipping it up behind them. Then he handed her a bag.

"Do I have all the items I'll need so I can clean up?" she asked.

"Yes," he gestured at the bag. "That's the restroom bag."

Amy nodded as she slung it over her shoulders.

"Want me to carry it?" he asked.

"Nah, I'm good." She smiled. "Let's go—I'm starving. Not to mention, dying to clean up. I feel pretty disgusting at this point."

They walked from their tent to the food stations at the edge of the esplanade where they'd witnessed the strange events last night. It was probably closer to lunchtime than breakfast now, but the smell of cooking food still lingered in the air. Perhaps they were serving brunch instead.

Amy's stomach started rumbling more ferociously the closer they got to the food. "Would you get me a plate?" she asked. "I need to go wash up first. I wonder what kind of amenities they have here?"

"Probably decent ones given the money someone appears to have spent on this place," Elijah said. "They might even have portable showers."

"In the desert?" Amy asked skeptically. She narrowed her eyes, curious how they'd even get showers out here.

"They could have brought in water tanks from Cairo. There are all sorts of possibilities. You'd be surprised the things people come up with in situations like this."

She shrugged. "I guess I would at that. Okay, I'll be back as quickly as I can."

Amy leaned in and gave Elijah a soft kiss, relieved when he didn't tense up or pull away. Then she walked the short distance to the ladies' area. Behind a privacy section marked off with hanging sheets, she did indeed find two portable showers. Elijah had been right; there was a good-sized water tank on wheels positioned just outside.

Beside a row of five port-a-potties was a makeshift cleaning station. There was a sign stating in several languages that if anybody needed soap, toothbrushes or toothpaste, they could get items in the medical tent, which was a red tent near the food station. That seemed very kind of them. Amy was more impressed now than ever by the generosity of whoever was funding this camp. They truly seemed to care about the people here.

Fortunately, though, Amy and Elijah had come prepared. Elijah—an old hand at traveling to remote places—knew exactly what they'd needed to bring along.

Amy used one of the port-a-potties and briefly considered trying out one of the showers, but there was a line for both of them. She didn't feel like waiting that long, so she used one of the three portable sinks that had small hoses attached, running from the water tank, she assumed. She dug into her bag and pulled out a bar of soap and a washcloth, then used the running water to wash herself, head to toe, as best she could. Next, she pulled out her toothbrush and toothpaste.

They had brought some dry shampoo along, not knowing if they'd have facilities for washing hair. She used the dry shampoo then picked out her tight red curls. Her hair was still going to be a disaster, but under the circumstances, who cared? She pulled it all up and twisted it into a messy bun. Problem solved.

Afterward, Amy felt somewhat more human. She put all her things back in her backpack and was on her way out of the cleaning station when she bumped into Shay, the teenager from the day before.

Shay smiled widely. "Hey, girl. How's it going? Did you find everything you needed?"

Her brown hair was pulled back in twin braids, and her tanned skin was starting to peel. Amy still had to fight a faint flush as she recalled the way she and Elijah had been fighting when Shay first approached them, but it didn't seem that the young woman held it against her.

"We're good," she said in reply. "Thanks. I think we're all set. Just going to get some food and then decide what we're doing today."

Shay nodded sagely. "Cool. You two gonna stick around for a while, then? I saw you talked to Snag last night."

A frown of confusion wrinkled Amy's forehead. "Snag?"

Shay tilted her head, birdlike. "Yeah, you know. The vamp. Mister 'Walks-Like-an-Egyptian?'"

Understanding dawned. "Oh. Uh... yeah. Sort of."

"Right. They call him Snag because of his..." Shay made a vague gesture toward her mouth, wiggling her finger up and down. "Anyway, are you staying?"

Amy blew out a breath. "I think so. For now, at least. Last night… definitely gave us some things to think about."

"I just bet it did." Shay grinned at her again. "Well, I'll leave you to it. Don't forget your sunscreen—your shoulders are starting to burn already. Have a good one!"

With a cheery wave, she departed, leaving Amy feeling like she'd been assaulted by a bubbly tornado. Amy shook her head and took off toward the food tents. Elijah was at one of the picnic tables nearby, two plates of food in front of him. As soon as she approached, he handed her a bottle of sunscreen.

"Be sure to put on plenty. You don't want to burn. Drink plenty of water today, too. Sunstroke would be terrible in your condition."

Amy smiled, taking the sunscreen and slathering everywhere she could reach with the lotion. "Get my back?" she asked, handing him the sunscreen and perching on the bench.

"Of course."

She held her hair up, and he smoothed the sunscreen over her back… or at least what was bare above her tank top. Elijah rubbed the lotion in with long, firm strokes, making her wish once again that he hadn't had his little freakout session in the tent earlier. She closed her eyes, appreciating the love and care in the slide of his fingers. Even with the false start this morning, something between them had changed for the better—she could feel it. She smiled at the thought.

Elijah's touch was surer. His words were softer. She could feel the weight of constant worry beginning to lift off her shoulders.

"There you go," Elijah said with a final caress across the back of her neck. "Now, eat something. I can hear your stomach growling."

She blushed—whether due to the brush of his fingertips or his words, she wasn't sure. They used napkins to wipe the slippery suntan lotion off their hands and dug into the food, which was a slightly different variation of beans and rice with vegetables and interesting spices. It was really rather good, and Amy thought she might have to look into some Middle Eastern recipes when they got back home.

When his plate was empty, Elijah cleared his throat as though unsure of what he was about to say. She raised her eyebrows at him, still chewing—urging him to go ahead.

He fiddled with his napkin and met her eyes. "I thought maybe I could take you exploring around the area later today. It's not as hot as it was yesterday, and there's more to see around Saqqara than just the Step Pyramid." He shrugged. "I mean… we're here anyway, so…"

She swallowed her mouthful of food. "I'd love that, Elijah. Would we need to find a car or get a taxi or something, though?"

Elijah shook his head. "No, I shouldn't think so. As long as we keep covered up and you continue to apply sun block with a trowel, it's all accessible on foot without too much problem." His enthusiasm grew at her receptive response, his hands moving as he spoke. "You saw how close Saqqara village is to this place? We could go into town long enough to pick up any supplies we need, and then there's a museum right on the boundary between the Nile floodplain and the edge of the desert."

She rested her elbows on the table next to her empty plate, growing intrigued. "A museum? Really? With artifacts and mummies and things?"

He nodded, his eyes glinting. "Yep. They've got a Ptolemaic mummy unearthed by Zahi Hawass, and part of the statue of the Pharaoh Djoser that came from this very complex. The inventory rotates in and out, but I think they've got a really impressive collection of tomb objects, too."

"I would absolutely kill to see that," Amy said, thrilled at the idea of a day spent exploring ancient art and history with her archaeologist husband.

A smile split Elijah's face. "Then, if there's time, there's also the Headless Pyramid and the Mastaba of Mereruka, both within half a mile of here with decent roads leading right up to them. Or we could do that another day—"

Her smile grew to match his. "This is going to be brilliant! I didn't even really think about all the things we could sightsee while we were here. And I've got the next best thing to a native guide! Okay, let's start by hitting the museum. Honestly, I think we're okay for supplies, since they seem to pretty much be providing everything we need here. So let's skip the village for now, and if there's time we can hike out to one of those other places you mentioned." Her brow crinkled. "Why do they call it the Headless Pyramid, anyway?"

She could tell he was warming to his subject. "It's more a place where a pyramid used to be, at this point," he said. "Picture the gap where a tooth used to be after someone pulled it out."

She wrinkled her nose at him. "I'd rather not," she said wryly.

He laughed. "Sorry. Basically, the superstructure is lost to time. It's gone. But the entrance to the underground tunnels and galleries is still there, and archaeologists have been excavating it in a serious way since 2008."

"Oooh." Amy waggled her fingers. "A ghost pyramid. Spooky."

Elijah's smile grew a bit frayed at the edges. "I'm guessing there's more woo-woo stuff going on right here than there will be at the unoccupied dig sites," he muttered.

It was clear he was still having significant issues with what they'd seen and experienced last night—not that Amy could blame him. Rather than risk falling back into a spat about what was going on here with the... supposed vampires... she moved the conversation along to practicalities.

"So, how about we hang out here for a few more hours until the sun gets a bit lower. We can nap, or chat with people—whatever, really. Then we'll hike out to the museum, and go from there?"

His expression cleared again. "Sure, babe. Whatever you want. This is your rodeo—I'm just along for the ride."

"Then we have a plan," she said, leaning forward to give him a peck on the lips. "I can hardly wait."

TEN

Elijah tagged along while Amy chatted with random people in the complex, reminding her every so often to reapply her sunscreen and drink more water. Despite the weirdness of the place, she seemed right at home here. The people they talked to ran the gamut from obvious new age hipster types to folks so normal that he wouldn't have given them a second glance in everyday circumstances.

They were on the receiving end of an additional smattering of crazy talk about supernatural creatures and a war between good and evil. But there were plenty of others here who seemed to be in roughly the same boat Amy was in—caught up in a questionable logic loop.

The world is crazy, and I need to do something.

This is something.

Therefore, I need to do this.

Elijah's air of detached superiority would be a lot easier to maintain if he hadn't watched a guy materialize from smoke and heard him speak telepathically inside his mind last night. For now, he was dealing with what he'd experienced by compartmentalizing it, which basically meant pretending it hadn't happened.

Even though it totally had.

He blew out a silent breath in frustration. In all fairness to Mister Wannabe Pharaoh, what he'd said had helped them with their problems. At least, it seemed to have done so. He and Amy had talked. Properly. They'd gone the better part of a day without fighting — more than that, they were *getting along*. Bonding. Enjoying each other's company.

A flush rose to Elijah's cheeks as he remembered how he'd started to *enjoy Amy's company* that morning in the tent, and he was glad that his dark skin hid it. That had rattled him, and he didn't think he'd done a very good job of hiding just how badly.

Fucking dream, he thought, only to blush harder as the unintentional double entendre registered.

The dream had been different this time, in a way that was completely and utterly devastating on several levels. First, it had gone on longer than in the past. Always before, he'd dreamed of walking in on Amy in another man's arms, and felt the sight making him horny as hell when he should have been angry, jealous, and hurt. It had only ever come to him in short fragments — abbreviated scenes with no context.

He'd always assumed it meant Amy had left him. It never occurred to him that he was supposed to join her and her lover — *her husband?* — like he'd done in the dream last night. Why would it? While it wasn't as though he'd never heard of alternative lifestyles, he'd always figured most swingers just paired off and did their thing in private with whatever partners they chose. This had been... something different than that.

He wished he could remember what they'd talked about in the dream, but the details had started to fade the moment he'd awoken to find himself grinding his dick against Amy's ass. There was a definite feeling of surreality to the whole thing. He was pretty sure the woman in the dream had borne no resemblance whatsoever to his red-haired, freckle-faced wife. But it had still somehow been Amy, without question.

Conversely, he really wished he *didn't* remember the man in the dream so well. Before, he'd always been a cipher. A faceless image for Elijah's mind to torment him with. Last night, the face had been the same one that poured itself into existence from a cloud of vapor, like some kind of high-end CGI special effect. Mister Wannabe Pharaoh, walking straight from his waking hallucinations into his dreams.

Fuck.

He needed to stop obsessing about this. It was a dream. Dreams were weird; that was kind of the point of them. This particular one probably said something really twisted about his current mental state, but... hey. Big surprise there, right?

Still, subconsciously wanting to have a threesome was probably less screwed up than getting off on your wife having an affair. Or at least it would have been less screwed up if he'd dreamed about getting it on with two women instead of his wife and another man. Another man who was her husband inside the dream, while Elijah had been—what?

They'll have need of a strong guardsman to watch over them. Fortunately, I know just the man for the job.

The snippet of dialogue flitted through Elijah's mind without context, and he shook his head, trying to rattle it loose.

He was fucking losing it, and he needed to stop. Things were going well right now. He couldn't afford to mess that up. They were going to go see some cool and interesting artifacts together, and even with all the people around, Amy had seemed pretty into the idea of having sex before Elijah had his little meltdown and ruined it. Maybe she'd be in the mood when they got back and went to bed.

Now, the sun was no longer pounding down on them from above. They'd retreated to the tent to rest for a while during the worst heat of the day, and Amy had dozed a bit. She stretched now, yawning widely.

"Hey, can we head out now?" she asked in a drowsy tone, unzipping the tent opening to peer outside.

"We sure can," he agreed readily. "Let's get kitted out and do it."

Her answering smile was as bright as the desert sky. "This is going to be *awesome.*"

He couldn't help smiling back, his earlier broodiness falling by the wayside as he looked forward to showing her some of the fruits of his colleagues' labors. Maybe someday soon, he would join them again in unearthing and restoring humanity's history. God knew, it was past time. The tentative hopeful feeling that had crept into his soul over the past day lifted its head again, making him feel lighter.

"You look like a kid contemplating a trip to the candy store," she accused, smirking at him.

He grinned back and splayed a hand over her belly where her shirt had ridden up, picturing a bouncy toddler with caramel skin running through aisles of sweets. "So do you," he shot back. "Now put on some more *SPF gazillion* and grab a long-sleeved shirt. I'll get your sun hat."

She stuck her tongue out at him, playful in a way he'd missed terribly in recent years, and they organized themselves for their mini-expedition. When they were ready, he hefted the larger of the packs—full of bottled water, more sunscreen, a compass, and some energy bars—while she took the lighter one. They headed toward the towering columns of the Grand Entrance, waving cheerily to a couple of people they'd chatted with earlier.

Instead of the Indian woman, Manisha, there was a tall white guy with brown hair and striking green eyes a similar shade to Amy's lounging on a folding chair near the colonnades. Those piercing eyes raked over both of them, assessing them with a single glance.

"Leaving us already?" he asked in an upper crust British accent.

Elijah stared right back, some of his earlier misgivings creeping in again. "Would it be a problem if we were?"

An eyebrow arched. "Not at all," he said, the mildness in his tone not reaching his green gaze.

"We merely like to keep track of how many people are staying here at any given time."

"'We'?" Amy echoed, stepping forward until her upper arm brushed Elijah's. "So you're another one of the... organizers?"

"Indeed I am," said the man, still unperturbed. "Necessity dictates that Manisha and I manage gate duty during the daylight hours. We tend to switch off around midday so we can each get some rest."

"You're aware that some of the people here claim you're vampires." Amy's voice was challenging, and Elijah was caught between wanting to cheer her on and wanting to cringe at the awkwardness of bringing something so ridiculous into the open.

The man snorted. "Of course I am."

"And are you?" Amy pressed. "A vampire, I mean?"

"Among other things, yes."

"Vampires don't exist," Elijah blurted, unable to stay silent after the matter-of-fact declaration.

"So one might assume," the man said. "And don't even get me started on werewolves or zombies."

Elijah blinked. "That's..." he began, only to flash back to the news reports about crowds of shambling 'survivors' after the bombing in Syria.

"Ridiculous?" the man finished for him. His lips stretched into a smile that bared pointed fangs for the space of a heartbeat, and his green eyes glowed with an actinic inner light for a moment before fading to normal. "Yes, quite so. Now... once again. Are you leaving us?"

Elijah's pulse thundered against his ribcage as a jolt of adrenaline shot through him—an instinctive fight or flight response to the presence of... what? A predator? A monster? Or... some kind of clever illusion?

Amy's voice was shaky, but she didn't back down as she said, "N-no. I came here to try and make a difference. I'm not leaving until I have more answers."

The man's expression sobered. "An admirable sentiment. Very well—I gather you're just heading out on a day trip, then?"

She nodded, and Elijah finally found his tongue. "Yes. Sightseeing for a few hours at the Imhotep Museum and possibly a couple of the closer dig sites. I'm a professor of archaeology. I've been out here before in a professional capacity."

The man's brows rose. "Archaeologist, eh? You should chat with Eris sometime. He used to be a tomb robber, and he probably lived through half of the stuff you've dug up. Him and Snag. Er, I mean *Menkhef*. I still can't get used to that." The last sentence was a barely audible mutter.

Elijah opened his mouth, but he wasn't sure what to say to that, so no words came out.

"Anyway, it sounds like you're well equipped to manage a short hiking expedition," the guy continued, waving a careless hand toward the exit from the complex. "We generally counsel people to be back by dark. The desert is an unforgiving landscape. That was true even before the world started going batshit insane."

"I know my way around the area," Elijah said. "We won't do anything unsafe."

The man's lips pulled into a pleasant smile, and this time there was no hint of pointed teeth. "Cheers. Have a lovely afternoon, both of you."

ELEVEN

The column-flanked entryway was no less impressive on the way out than it had been on the way in yesterday, but Amy was too focused on the conversation they'd just had to pay much attention to it. The British guy... he'd had fangs. Like... *proper fangs*.

"It could have been another trick. But what's their game?" Elijah muttered, as though reading her mind. He was clearly as rattled as she was, if not more so.

"Elijah... we watched a man materialize right in front of us. In the middle of a crowd, no less—not on some stage like an illusionist or a magician in Las Vegas."

"This stuff is impossible," Elijah said, still sounding dazed. "You've got a background in the sciences just like I do, Ames. You *know* it's impossible."

"I know what I saw," Amy shot back. "You saw the same thing or you wouldn't be so freaked out right now."

He was silent for a moment before he shook his head almost angrily. "This place is fucking mental. I swear I'm getting to the bottom of things before we leave."

That's the spirit, Amy thought. *Stubbornness for the win!*

"I'm on board with that," she said.

He let out a frustrated sigh. "At least they seem to be telling the truth about letting people leave if they want to. Let's just go and enjoy the museum. We can worry about the rest later."

She nodded, trying to put the unsettling revelations aside in favor of this opportunity for bonding time. "Sure. How far away is it, anyway?"

The mid-afternoon sun was at their backs as they emerged from the covered entrance. Elijah pointed east, toward the line of green visible in the distance. "It's right on the edge of the Nile floodplain. Barely half a mile."

They headed off, and Amy was immediately grateful for her sunhat even in the slanting afternoon light. Before long, an attractive sandstone building landscaped with palm trees became visible, and less than fifteen minutes later, they were walking up to the shaded portico covering the tall double doors of the entrance.

The place seemed deserted, but for all Amy knew, that was normal. After all, this was a fairly remote area next to a tiny village. From what Elijah had described, Saqqara mostly housed workers who assisted in area digs. The pop-up commune they'd just left probably represented the most excitement this place had seen in millennia.

Elijah grasped the handle of one of the big doors and tugged, but it remained stubbornly closed. He tried the other — same result.

"That's odd," he said.

Amy frowned. A sign next to the doors listed the opening times in English and Arabic, and the place wasn't due to close for two hours. "Did we miss a sign about it being closed for renovations or something?"

"No, we didn't. This is the main entrance—if it's closed, it should say so." Elijah gave a final tug on the doors and stepped back. "Well, then. So much for the first part of my romantic date idea."

She laughed. "Best laid plans, right? We're really close to the village here, aren't we? Why don't we walk to the nearest shop that sells cold soda and ask if they know anything about when it's going to reopen?"

"Might as well." Elijah shrugged and shot her a crooked smile. "But, *soda*, Ames? You know that stuff will rot your teeth, right?"

"Smartass." She poked his arm in retaliation for the old joke. "Which way?"

He caught her hand, lacing their fingers together. "The village is literally right behind the museum. There used to be a sort of general convenience store a few blocks away, when I was here before. Newspapers, snacks, gasoline—that kind of thing."

"Perfect," she said, and let him lead her back to the road abutting the museum parking lot. "You know, it seems kind of odd that the lot is totally empty. Shouldn't there at least be security guards on duty? There's valuable stuff here, after all."

"Yeah, there should be. Who knows, though? They could have walked or biked to work from the village." He gave her hand a squeeze. "We'll see if anyone knows what's up. A lot of the people here speak at least a bit of English or French. It helps them find work at the dig sites."

As they walked into the greener area of Saqqara village, they found it was also surprisingly empty.

"Good lord, this place is like a ghost town. I thought you said people lived here?" Amy asked, surprised.

"Uh... they do?" He posed it like a question, sounding suddenly unsure. "I've never seen it so deserted. Everyone seems to have closed up shop and gone home."

"Okay, that's a little creepy."

He chewed on his lip for a moment. "Let's head toward the store. If anything seems dodgy, we'll go back."

Amy nodded in agreement despite the nagging feeling growing inside her that this whole excursion had been a really bad idea. They held hands as they walked down the empty street. The low brick and stucco buildings lining the pavement on both sides were all closed and sealed up tightly. The sense of foreboding lingered in her chest, becoming more difficult to ignore the longer they walked through the deserted town.

"Hey, look over there!" Amy pointed ahead of them. A few blocks away, a group of people was moving down a side street, heading away from them.

"Finally!" Elijah said with relief. "Huh. Maybe there's a festival or some kind of religious holiday going on today. That could explain why all the shops and the museum are closed."

He studied the pack of people. The ones in front were turning down another side road that would soon take them out of sight.

"Hello there!" he called. Several of the people near the back of the group halted and turned toward them, but did not answer. "*Bonjour?*" he tried next, in hopes that any of them spoke French.

The group stayed still—staring at them, but apparently not interested enough to respond to the greeting. After a few tense moments, they turned and continued on their path, disappearing around the corner of a building.

Amy let out a nervous laugh. "Okay. *That* wasn't unsettling or anything. I guess the creepy Egyptian gang members don't want to be our friends today." She tightened her grip on Elijah's hand. "Can we, uh, leave now, please?"

He continued to stare after the group for a long moment before shaking himself free of his short reverie. "Yeah. Sure thing, Ames. I have no idea what that was about, but we can go check out the mastaba, at least. That way the afternoon won't be a complete write-off. It's within reasonable walking distance, and the roads should be well marked. There's some extraordinary artwork inside the interior chambers, and I brought a flashlight with extra batteries so we won't be in the dark."

"Sounds good. Let's get going—this place is seriously starting to creep me out." Amy didn't relinquish her grip on Elijah's hand. The excitement of sightseeing had worn off, replaced with an irrational certainty that bad things were about to happen. It was ridiculous. So what if the museum and shops were closed? Like Elijah had said, it was probably the Egyptian version of a bank holiday.

In a place as small as this, they must just close up everything and gather someplace centrally located to do their thing. The group they'd seen could have been heading toward the local mosque or community center or whatever, and maybe none of them spoke English or French. They probably didn't want to deal with a couple of clueless foreigners when they were late to... wherever they were going. That was totally normal, right?

The weight in her chest grew heavier.

A stiff, heated breeze gusted past them, carrying with it traces of sand, dry air, and a faint, rotting stench that turned Amy's stomach sour—roadkill, maybe. Faint as it was, she couldn't help but notice. It was probably down to her pregnancy. Hormones seemed to have heightened all her senses recently.

Amy swallowed against the nausea, contemplating the reason why so many people had flocked to the peace enclaves in the first place. She usually felt safe with Elijah—it was one of many things she loved about him. He was tall and intimidating enough that most people wouldn't mess with him. He also gave off a sort of vibe when he was with people that he cared about—one that said no one had better mess with them, or they'd answer to him. She'd jokingly called him her silent bodyguard on more than one occasion.

Right now, she appreciated that feeling more than she could say, but it still wasn't enough to stop the creeping dread rising inside her. She clung

to Elijah's hand, following him back to the museum
and the desert beyond.

TWELVE

For Menkhef, meditation had never been a particularly effective balm. Perhaps it had something to do with spending millennia aware of his surroundings while being unable to move or interact with the outside world in any way. Perhaps it was because during much of that time — and the centuries that followed — his sanity had been... *intermittent.*

Whatever the case, meditation wasn't a skill he had nearly as much experience with as most people might assume, and it also wasn't a skill that was proving to be of much help to him now.

Ever since coming across the unhappy married couple the previous evening, he had been beset by memories best left forgotten. Normally, he avoided the nightmares of his distant past via the simple expedient of not sleeping. It had always struck him as an elegant solution, despite Eris' occasional pitying looks when the subject came up.

Now, whenever his focus wavered, visions of corrosive black smoke and the screams of loved ones pricked at the edges of his awareness. By rights, after more than four millennia, the look of devastation on Heqab's face as he stood over Nebetta's broken body with a spear pointed at Menkhef's heart should have faded under the ravages of time.

Yes, the demon's sibilant voice had crooned, the dark fog swirling ecstatically around them. *Kill your ruler, insect, and die for it. Kill him and make him mine!*

Menkhef remembered stalking forward until Heqab's spearpoint pricked his chest, blood trickling from the wound in a thick, red rivulet. Bloodlust would have driven him to impale himself on the wooden shaft, if that was what it took to reach the thundering pulse of the man on the other end with his fangs, but the spear clattered to the ground before the point could slide between his ribs. Heqab followed its trajectory an instant later, crumpling to kneel next to the bloody corpse of the woman they'd both loved.

"I cannot kill you," he said, his voice scraped raw by grief and the bitter acid of the fog. "I will not kill you, Menkhef… not even for this. I beg of you—don't make me live with that decision for another moment."

Heqab's right hand had rested on the still place between Nebetta's breasts where her heart had beaten mere moments before—a tender gesture. It was sticky with the blood from her torn throat. Menkhef fell upon the man who had been his closest friend and companion since boyhood, with no thought for anything beyond slaking the terrible, burning thirst that clawed at his body like a thousand ravenous jackals. Warrior that he was, Heqab uttered no cry as Menkhef's fangs sank into salty skin, coppery ambrosia exploding from the jagged tears in his neck.

Menkhef blinked, pulling himself free of the sucking pit of the past... yet again. Around him, the tomb in which the Pharaoh Qahedjet had sealed him swam into focus, the painted carvings blurred by time. An electric bulb threw harsh yellow light around the chamber.

His lips thinned. Fortunately, his mental shields had sprung up out of habit as visions from the past rose inside him. Even so, his preoccupation interfered with his duties toward the souls in his care—both those above in Djoser's pyramid complex, and those hiding with him in the depths of the South Tomb.

Unacceptable.

He was supposed to be watching over them, not wallowing in bitter memory. Perhaps he was not giving the humans enough credit, with his insistence on projecting calm over the area. Yet now that their minds had become receptive to his, he could all too easily flood them with his nightmare of death and loss should his shields slip at an inopportune moment.

Not to mention the effect it would have on his fellow vampires if they realized that he was weakening. He'd been surprised on a very deep level at the way the others had deferred to his leadership after Eris drank from them and used their combined powers to revive him from his state of near death. Even Tré, who for centuries had led and forged the vampires into a cohesive group, merely stepped back and focused his efforts on organizing Menkhef's vision for this place and the others like it around the world.

That was true leadership—a fire in which Menkhef, too, had been forged at a young age. The life of a true leader was steeped in service, not tyranny. A true leader ate only after the lowest of his followers had eaten; slept only once those in his care were safe and protected; never sent another to do something he was not himself willing to do.

In life, he had not always been such a leader to his people… though he had striven to act in their best interests to the extent that his imperfect nature allowed. In undeath, he had hidden behind a cloak of guilt and madness for longer than many civilizations existed—but now, the moment of truth was upon him.

He merely had to avoid being brought low by a bare moment's interaction with a pair of humans, for the sole reason that they reminded him of his lost mates. When he'd touched them, he had allowed himself an instant of foolish hope. But, truly, what were the odds that Heqab and Nebetta would be reborn after four millennia to marry each other and conveniently present themselves before Menkhef, right above the tomb where he'd been buried?

No spark of connection had flared along his nerve endings when he touched them. They were merely a troubled couple, drawn to a faraway place in hopes of finding answers. Perhaps the ones he'd offered would make a difference to them in some small way.

He hoped so. For whatever reason, their brokenness called to his on a very deep level.

A sense of worry not his own brushed the edges of the bond he shared with the other vampires, and he lowered his shields to feel it more clearly. It was Chan Wei Yong, the young man he'd so recently utilized to deliver a message in Kuala Lumpur. Duchess' mate.

I think I need some help here. The worry grew deeper, tinged with a flash of real fear. *It's Marie.*

A quick image of Duchess staring into the distance, her blue eyes glazed and unseeing, flitted across Menkhef's awareness. Now the others' concern joined Chan's. Menkhef rose smoothly from the mat on which he'd been kneeling and swept out of the room, transforming into mist and swirling through the maze of corridors separating his tomb from the quarters Duchess and Chan had claimed.

He arrived to find that Oksana and Mason had beaten him here. The physician knelt at Duchess' side and gently turned her face toward the light. Her eyelids were fluttering now, eyes rolling up until only the whites showed. Menkhef probed at her shields, but her mind was far away, locked down tight.

"How long has she been like this?" Mason asked, peeling back one of her eyelids with a frown.

Chan stood a step away, tension coiled in his spine, his arms crossed tightly in front of him. "I'm not sure. I went to get us a couple of blood bags from the storage unit, and when I got back she was unresponsive. I tried calling her name and shaking her, but I didn't want to get more creative without knowing what the hell's happening to her."

Oksana had hung back, standing close to the door. She, too, looked as tense as a drawn bowstring. "She's in a trance. A deep one. I can't even feel her right now."

Tré's deep voice came across the link. *Do you want the rest of us to come, or stay out from underfoot?*

I will deal with her, Menkhef assured. *Stay alert.*

"Can you jolt her out of it, Snag?" Oksana asked.

Mason glanced up from his examination. "Since you're the most powerful, you might as well try. Medically, I'm at a loss—we didn't cover psychic vampire trances at uni."

Menkhef focused his power and crashed through the reflective wall around Duchess' thoughts. Visions pulsed through the breach, passing from her mind to his. At the same moment Menkhef saw what had pulled Duchess' awareness away from her body, she startled awake, returning to consciousness with a gasp.

"The undead," she whispered. "They're coming."

-o-o-o-

Menkhef's failure to police his own mind had resulted in a breach that could easily have had devastating consequences if Duchess' own well-developed mental powers had not sensed the approach of Bael's undead forces. As the other vampires gathered for a council of war, he cast his awareness outward—beyond the confines of Djoser's complex to the surrounding landscape.

There, as Duchess had seen, lay a dark stain where the inhabitants of the nearby village had been not half a day before. Some of the local residents had already come to the step pyramid upon learning of the vampires' presence. Many others had remained in the town, not wishing to sleep in tents in the desert when their comfortable homes were such a short distance away.

With luck, some would have fled, and others might have escaped Bael's mindless minions by hiding. He mourned those that had been lost with a deep ache of regret and a sense of failure.

"You couldn't have known," Duchess said. She was seated on the mattress she shared with her mate, hugging her drawn-up knees. "There was no way to foresee when and how the Darkness would rally to engage us. We've been here for weeks with no sign of them."

The room was crowded with all eleven vampires inside. It was not yet dusk, but Xander had left some of the trusted humans from his business in London to watch over things aboveground while they discussed strategy. Duchess, Chan, Oksana, and Mason were seated on the room's bare mattress while the others stood at intervals along the walls.

Tré's mate Della crossed her arms. "Does this mean the person you lost is nearby, Snag?" she asked. "Did the undead come because they sensed your proximity to your mate?"

Eris saved him from having to come up with an answer to a question that could not be answered. "Speaking as someone who's spent the last several centuries being regularly trounced at chess, this feels more like an endgame than a vortex of chaos to me."

"It's true that things have been unexpectedly peaceful until now," Tré agreed. "And it's not as though Bael could have failed to notice where we've been holed up."

"Yeah, we're kind of the opposite of a secret at this point," Trynn put in. "Kovac can't have missed all the chatter online about the enclaves."

"Speaking of which," Tré continued, "we need to contact the other locations and warn them that the undead may be moving on them as well."

"Already on it," said Xander. "The satellite link is holding, so I've got Shay on a group Skype with Madame Francine in New Orleans, Mama Lovelie in Haiti, Trynn's old boss Mandy in Canada, Mason's brother in Singapore, and HelioTeque's VP in London. Between them, they'll disseminate the information to the other locations."

"Which leaves one very important question," Manisha said softly. "What are we going to do when the undead show up here in force?"

"Fight them," Chan said simply, not moving from his position crouched next to Duchess with his arm around her shoulders.

It will not be so simple as that, Menkhef sent, the tiredness that had plagued him for days now returning in force.

"Then what exactly do you suggest, sir?" Chan retorted, his military background and hawkish response to the approaching threat reminding

Menkhef for a piercing, painful moment of his long lost and much beloved captain of the guard.

For now, reconnaissance, he said evenly.

Eris crossed his arms, meeting Menkhef's gaze with his gold-flecked one. "But first, a bit of sharing and caring. Della asked you about your mate, and your failure to answer is no longer acceptable. The time for secrets between us is fast coming to a close, old friend."

Menkhef held Eris' eyes for a long moment, reluctantly examining the motivation behind his lack of transparency regarding a subject that affected all of them. Allowing a small measure of the tension in his shoulders to loosen, he met the others' eyes one at a time.

The Council has thirteen members, he reminded them pointedly.

Xander raised an eyebrow. "We're aware," he said, his voice as dry as the dusty landscape above them. "And we thought that Sangye was our odd vampire out, but then he died." Next to him, Manisha gave a minute flinch, and he wrapped her hand in his. "Though, mind you, Duchess told us you'd already said that he wasn't the thirteenth, so…" He trailed off, and blinked. "Oh." He blinked again. "*Oh.* You have got to be *kidding.* Bloody hell, Snag. *Really?* I didn't think you had it in you."

"Where's a decoder ring when you need one?" Della asked. "Someone spell it out, please?"

Eris was still holding Menkhef's gaze, unwavering. "When Bael came for him, our taciturn friend had not one lover, but two."

Della's eyes went wide. "You had a *harem*? Was that even a thing in ancient Egypt?"

I did not have a harem, he replied evenly.

Trynn gave him a shrewd look. "But when Bael came, two people sacrificed for you; not just one. Is that why you're so powerful?"

I do not know, he told her truthfully. *Whatever the case, the point is moot. There is no indication that either of those I lost is nearby. I have made a point to greet all newcomers as they arrive. I have touched all of them, and never felt the flare of the bond that the rest of you have experienced.*

"Do you think the two of them somehow found each other across their reincarnations?" Manisha asked quietly. "Do you believe they're together somewhere?"

He paused for a long moment. *I hope so.*

"All right," Tré said, interrupting the heavy atmosphere. "While this is undoubtedly important information to have, for now we need to focus on the immediate threat."

"I'll shift into wolf form and sneak into the village to see what's happening," Manisha said.

"*We'll* shift into wolf form and sneak into the village to see what's happening," Xander corrected without missing a beat. "You're not going alone, and since we're the only ones who can do it before the sun goes down I suppose it makes sense."

Manisha nodded, not arguing.

"That will leave the complex essentially unguarded for more than an hour until the sun goes down," Chan pointed out. "Xander, can your people topside handle that?"

"Yes," Xander said. His eyes flicked to Snag. "Though it would be useful if you could start pumping out the mental happy juice again. You've been… a bit on edge the past few hours, and it's coming across through your powers, old chap."

Menkhef nodded, well aware that he had shirked his self-appointed responsibilities.

"There's another option," Della said. "Could we fit all of the humans down here in the tunnels? It might be safer for them when…" She swallowed. "When things start to get ugly."

Tré's mouth twitched down. "It might. Or it might trap them with nowhere to retreat."

"If we can't protect them, they'll be dead either way," Chan said bluntly. "I've seen what this creature—this *demon*—can do, and if he gets to them, being in a tunnel isn't going to make a blind bit of difference versus standing on open ground."

"We'll go and get a better idea of what we're up against," Manisha said. "That should help when it comes to planning a response."

Tré nodded, his gaze taking in both her and Xander. "Go. But I want you both to stay out of sight and maintain mental contact the entire time."

"We should inform the humans of the danger," Duchess said. "At least let them know not to leave the compound. We could give them the choice of coming down here or staying aboveground, where they can try to flee if need be."

"Xander," Tré began, "do we know if all the people here are currently accounted for?"

"All but two of them are," Xander said. "Two individuals and a family of four left this morning—

hopefully they all went straight to Cairo and avoided whatever happened in the village. But there was a married couple that left to sightsee at the museum and the local digs a couple of hours ago. They were a fairly distinctive pair—a tall back man and pale, red-haired woman."

A chill of unease washed through Menkhef's chest, and Xander gave him a surprised look.

Search for them while you are out, he managed, pressing down on the irrational reaction.

"We will," Manisha said, her dark eyes shining with concern for the innocent humans.

"Of course," Xander agreed. "I'll brief Shay and the HelioTeque employees about what's happening on our way out." His green eyes sought Menkhef's again. "Remember to think calm thoughts, old man."

It was Tré who answered him. "Thank you, *tovarăş*. Be careful—both of you."

Xander gave his friend a nod and a tight smile before following Manisha out of the crowded room.

THIRTEEN

When nothing else weird or unsettling happened after they left the village and headed back into the desert, Amy gradually started to relax. The Mastaba of Mereruka was every bit as amazing as Elijah had made it sound. It, too, had been deserted, but unlike the museum no effort had been made to bar access to the interior.

The outside might have been a bit underwhelming, but once she'd passed through the entrance to Mereruka's tomb, her breath had exited her lungs in a shocked gasp. The chambers were a landscape of statues and artwork that brought a long-dead world back to vibrant life. By the time they'd made the rounds and left the place, Amy felt like she had slipped back in time to a land both simpler and more complex.

She could practically feel the sway of a fishing boat beneath her feet... hear the clash of battling chariots... the scratch of a scribe's stylus... the low chanting of priests conducting a religious ceremony. Unbidden, the bronze-lit eyes of the mysterious man who'd greeted them at the pyramid complex swam before her vision. His high cheekbones, his straight nose, the strong jut of his chin, and the touch of gray at his temples combined to awaken an ache in her chest that made no sense.

He'd been an impossibility, true. Materializing from a swirl of fog, as out of place in the modern world as could be, but perfectly suited to his time-worn surroundings in the shadow of the step pyramid. Even so, they'd only interacted for a handful of moments. Why should she be any more fixated on him than on the strikingly handsome green-eyed Brit who'd flashed a vampire's fangs at them before wishing them a pleasant afternoon?

And why the hell was she focused on *any* other man right now when this was her chance to finally make things right with the guy she loved more than life itself? Elijah should be the center of her attention today, not some creature who might well drink human blood the same way she guzzled Dr. Pepper. She firmed her grip on Elijah's hand, dragging her attention back to the present and the tumble of stone blocks ahead of them.

Elijah pointed with his free hand. "That's it. The Headless Pyramid. We should have time for a quick look around and still be able to get back before dark."

She tilted her head at the gap in the desert landscape. "Okay… I'll admit this is almost the opposite of what I was expecting."

He chuckled. "I tried to warn you. Missing tooth, remember? This is what happens when you take the pyramid away and leave behind only what was hidden beneath it."

Indeed, what was left was a sunken pit with random piles of stone blocks resting here and there. A couple of areas were fenced off with wooden boards, and as they got closer, she could see that those safety fences surrounded dark holes in the ground.

"What happened to the rest of it?" she asked. It was interesting to be able to see the tunnels and shafts that would normally be hidden from view by the stone superstructure of a pyramid, but it was also a bit disconcerting.

Elijah shrugged. "Good question. My guess is that someone in the distant past wanted to save time and money by reusing the dressed stone for another building project, and they were willing to risk their gods' wrath to do it."

"Makes sense," Amy allowed. "Bronze Age recycling, right?"

He laughed again, a sound Amy didn't hear nearly often enough these days. She let the last of her tension from earlier slip away and just enjoyed the evening. The sun was slipping low in the sky, the temperature growing cooler as it did. She pulled off her sunhat and folded it up, jamming it in her back pocket. The faint breeze felt divine against her sweaty scalp.

They still had many things to face. Elijah's depression, the threat to his job security, her pregnancy... not to mention the small matter of the world falling apart around them. Right now, though, she was in an amazing location with someone she loved, under a wide blue sky turning to shades of scarlet and magenta in the west. She let Elijah guide her down a ramp-like structure made of rubble and packed dirt that led into the excavated area where the pyramid had once been.

They didn't have the equipment to explore the deep shafts leading down to the underground tomb areas, and looking at the dark pits behind the makeshift fences, Amy didn't think she would have wanted to, regardless. But Elijah led her around and pointed out the remnants of the original structure, and she found herself getting wrapped up in his obvious enthusiasm for a subject close to his heart. Whatever else happened, she vowed there and then that she would convince him to start going on digs again.

The lower edge of the brilliant orange sun had just touched the horizon when Elijah stilled beside her, looking back toward the ramp they'd used to enter the site. She frowned and followed his gaze, only to find a group of people dressed in the kind of loose, white clothing favored by the natives approaching.

They were... *shambling*. There was really no other word to use.

"Are those the same people we saw in the village earlier?" she asked slowly.

Elijah's hand tightened around hers, the grip almost painful.

"Ames," he said very deliberately, "please tell me the heat's getting to me and I'm seeing things."

She looked more closely at the figures, a trickle of cold dread twining through her chest until it felt like it might choke her. The people approaching the edge of the pit were gray-skinned, with sunken features. Some of them looked blind, their eyes milky and unseeing. Others had... limbs missing. Grotesque, unhealed injuries that should have been debilitating… if not deadly.

"Elijah." Amy's voice was a hoarse croak as panic slammed into her. "We need to get out of here."

The tendons in Elijah's jaw stood out, flexing in agitation as he threw a quick, searching gaze around their surroundings. Amy did the same, the fine hair at the back of her neck prickling as she confirmed what they both already knew. The… *things*… were blocking their only means out of the excavated pit. Aside from the ramp, everything else was smooth earth and stone, easily eight feet high and with no obvious hand- or footholds.

"*Shit*," Elijah hissed under his breath, moving to place Amy behind him.

"We have to get away from them," Amy whispered, all the sensationalized news reports from Syria flooding into her mind.

Elijah released her hand and stooped to pick up a loose chunk of rock about twice the size of his fist. "See if you can find a place to climb out," he said as the first of the creatures stumbled down the ramp, its fellows following close on its heels. "Maybe you can pile up some rubble to stand on or something. Don't let them get close to you. It doesn't look like they move very fast."

Amy's heart pounded with terror. The breeze wafted a horrible stench of rotting flesh across her face, nearly making her gag.

"Go!" Elijah barked, and she tore her legs free from their paralysis.

It was hopeless—she knew that before she'd even started. They had a clear view of the walls of the pit, and any rubble large enough to be useful for climbing out would also be too heavy to move. Nonetheless, she started a quick, systematic survey of the outer walls, throwing nervous glances over her shoulder every few seconds to check on Elijah.

He was trying to talk to them—backing slowly away from their advance as he spoke to them in English, French, then Spanish. It was obvious even from across the length of the pit that there was nothing behind those dead, filmy eyes, however. Nothing except bloodlust, at any rate. One of the creatures reached a ragged hand toward Elijah, making Amy gasp with fear on his behalf. Elijah knocked it away violently and hurled the large rock he was holding at its head.

The blow was a direct hit, and the thing staggered—only to right itself, unfazed by a blow that should have rendered it unconscious at the very least. Amy swallowed a sob of fear and started praying, still searching feverishly for some means of escape for them.

"Get out however you can and *run*, Amy!" Elijah called. "Don't wait for me!"

Oh hell no, was her only thought as the dozen or so creatures ranged around Elijah and started driving him backward—driving him toward one of the open shafts, with its rickety wooden safety fence. They were *toying with him*.

Ignoring his barked order, she grabbed a couple of heavy rocks and threw them at the advancing creatures, scooping up more as she ran toward them. They were losing the light, making the uneven, rock-strewn footing ridiculously dangerous, but the thought of what might happen if they got too close to Elijah and overwhelmed him lent her feet wings.

"I told you to go!" Elijah shouted as she reached him, real fear audible in his voice for the first time as he clenched his jaw and grabbed the largest rocks he could lift, hurling them at the nearest zombies.

"Not happening," she grated, trying to help him hold back the advancing tide with her smaller missiles.

It wasn't working.

A frantic glance found that they were nearly backed up against the rickety fence with a yawning black chasm beyond. Just then, the eerie, unexpected howl of a wolf broke the tense silence, echoed a moment later by a second. They sounded close.

The creatures surrounding them paused, looking around as if in confusion, their milky eyes scanning the deepening dusk. Two large, gray, four-legged blurs burst into the pit and plowed into the fight, ripping and tearing at anything within reach.

Amy screamed in surprise at the sudden carnage, the sound torn from her throat. The giant wolves continued to attack the undead monsters surrounding her and Elijah, and she wasn't sure whether to be more frightened now, or less. Her answer came a moment later, when one of the zombies armed with a broken length of wood slammed it into the side of Elijah's head, sending him crashing through the flimsy barrier around the excavation shaft.

Amy shrieked *"No!"* and dove after him, grabbing his forearm with both hands as he hung by his fingertips from the dusty edge of the drop-off.

FOURTEEN

The sun was slipping under the horizon above the South Tomb. Menkhef was aware of its passage even without being able to see it—tied as all vampires were to its fiery push and pull. He allowed the knowledge to slide over the surface of his consciousness in favor of concentrating on the blanket of calm that he, Eris, and Duchess were attempting to maintain for the humans above them.

Menkhef cast another part of his mind farther across the desert and the fertile Nile valley east of them, unwilling to make the same mistake twice by focusing too much on the compound. The details were unclear; too much of his attention was taken up by other things to see all that he wished to see. Still, he could tell that the undead were moving... but not *en masse*. Not yet.

Several of the other vampires were here, offering their life force through the bond to help bolster the three with the greatest psychic abilities. Mason had gone to speak with the young human woman who'd been communicating electronically with the other enclaves, but he entered now, his aura grim. Menkhef drew enough of his awareness back to his body to open his eyes and focus on the physician.

"Those creatures are massing around all of the other worldwide locations as well," Mason said, his voice tight with worry. "They're not doing anything aggressive yet—just gathering nearby—like a bloody noose tightening."

"Things are coming to a head," Oksana said, sounding just as tense.

Mason paced, his arms crossed. "We need a better plan than this. None of the other enclaves have vampires to keep the people calm in the face of rampaging zombies. There will be panic."

Tré's deep voice was calm, but sober. "If we don't gain some sort of edge for the final battle, panic will be the least of their problems. There will be a slaughter."

Mason rounded on Tré, his fists clenched. "My brother is running one of those enclaves, Tré. My *baby nieces* are there!"

Enough, Menkhef said calmly, letting power flow through the bond. *The stakes are the same no matter where our loved ones shelter. Bael will not rest until the entire world is broken beneath him. Not unless we defeat him first.*

Mason turned the glare towards him. "Not helping, mate," he said through clenched teeth.

Before the pointless argument could continue, Xander's mental voice cut sharply across the link. *Snag! We found your missing humans. Eleven undead are attacking them at an excavation site half a mile northeast of the complex. We're going in, but we need reinforcements right the fuck now!*

A mental map of the area appeared in Menkhef's head, and he was on his feet instantly, pinning the others with his eyes.

Oksana, Chan — with me, quickly. Tré —

Tré nodded his understanding. "The rest of us will watch over the compound. Go."

Menkhef did not spare a reply, instead transforming into mist between one breath and the next, streaking toward the entrance to the tomb complex and the desert above. He quickly outdistanced the two younger vampires, speeding toward the location of the tomb that had once belonged to the Pharaoh Menkauhor.

The sense of foreboding that had plagued him since learning that the human couple had wandered from the complex returned in force, becoming a nearly all-consuming need to be at the site of the battle *now*. The desert landscape flew past in a blur as he pushed himself to the limit.

He crossed the kilometer or so separating the two sites in mere moments. Ahead, his sense of the undead pricked at his awareness, their twisted wrongness acting like a beacon as sure as any lighthouse. He materialized in the open pit where the battle was taking place just in time to see one of the unnatural creatures strike the dark-skinned human man, sending him crashing through a flimsy barrier and into the open shaft beyond.

The woman screamed and dove after him, all thoughts of defending herself forgotten in her desperation to reach her husband. Menkhef lunged into the midst of the confusion, batting away two of the creatures before they could grasp her. He was aware of Chan and Oksana arriving and joining the fight as Xander and Manisha's wolves continued to tear at whatever attackers they could reach.

Menkhef reached out for the sense of the humans' minds and found the man dazed from a head wound, wavering on the knife's edge of consciousness. He wouldn't be able to pull himself up, and the woman wouldn't be able to hold onto him if his grip on the crumbling edge of the shaft slipped.

Judging that the others could hold back the remaining undead for a few moments, Menkhef dematerialized and swirled into the open shaft. Centering himself, he wrapped his vaporous form around the man's body, transforming it into the same incorporeal form long enough to transport him away from of the excavation area.

Behind them, he heard the woman scream, "Elijah!" as she felt her husband's arm dissolving within her grasp. The noise would draw more of the undead toward her. Menkhef placed the man on the ground a short distance away and swooped back into the pit, swirling past the creatures threatening her and plucking her away to safety as well.

He materialized them next to her husband. She staggered on unsteady legs, her eyes darting wildly from him to the man's crumpled form. "*What—*" she began in a high-pitched, frightened voice.

Menkhef eased her down to a seated position, steadying her with one hand. With the other, he reached to tilt the dark-skinned man's face to one side, intending to examine the wound at his temple. As though a circuit had connected the instant he touched both of them at once, a powerful shock barreled through Menkhef's body, sending him reeling backward to land unceremoniously on his rump in the sand.

-o-o-o-

Menkhef knew his mouth was hanging open. The man — *Heqab, the man was Heqab!* — stirred, and the woman — *oh, my Nebetta!* — stared at him, wide-eyed. Menkhef stared right back at her, dumbfounded.

"My heart," he whispered, voice hoarse from long disuse. His eyes tore away to look at the man. *"My soul.* After all this time…"

Before either of them could respond to such a ridiculous declaration from someone they would consider a complete stranger, Chan jogged up, grim-faced.

"We're too exposed here," he said without preamble, and just like that, the moment snapped like a broken thread.

"Yes," Menkhef agreed, and suddenly he was not acting like the most powerful vampire in existence, but rather like a fool sitting on his backside in the dust, staring at a pair of humans with his jaw hanging slack.

Chan looked between the three of them warily. "Can… these two travel, sir?" he asked slowly, as if to an imbecile.

Through the bond, Menkhef could feel Oksana, Manisha, and Xander's curiosity. He tamped everything down, shaping it into a hard, burning ball, and drew heavy layers of practicality over it.

I will transport Heq —

He cut himself off and tried again. *I will transport the man. The rest of you can escort the woman back on foot. She is uninjured, but shock is a possibility.*

Oksana and the two wolves joined them, a quick visual sweep assuring Menkhef that any injuries they'd sustained while dispatching the undead were superficial. He first met Oksana's eyes, and then Xander's lupine gaze, aware of the picture he must present, but relying on whatever regard they might hold for him after their years of camaraderie.

"Guard her from harm at all costs," he begged them in hoarse tones.

Snag, Xander's mental voice began, but Menkhef cut him off.

"*All costs,*" he repeated.

Xander's furry head cocked in consternation, but Oksana laid a hand on the wolf's shoulder and he subsided.

"We have her," Oksana said. "Go. We'll join you soon."

Relief at the younger vampire's understanding flooded Menkhef, and he nodded. He pushed himself up from the ground on shaking arms and legs, giving the red-haired woman a final, lingering look. Then he gathered up the dazed man at his feet and swirled a cloak of power around them both, disappearing into the rapidly cooling desert night as fast-moving vapor.

FIFTEEN

"Elijah!" Amy cried as her husband disappeared right before her disbelieving eyes. Fresh panic flooded her and she cast around, her eyes sliding wildly over the pretty black woman, the Asian man, and the two wolves—*wolves!*—arrayed around her.

"What. The. *Hell!*" she shouted, each word louder than the last.

The Asian guy frowned, glancing from side to side as though he expected more zombies to appear out of nowhere and jump on them. The wolves looked restless as well. Amy staggered upright from her undignified sprawl in the sand, nearly toppling over when her legs didn't want to hold her.

The woman stepped forward as though to steady her. Amy stumbled backward, out of reach, and locked her knees to stay upright. Her gaze was drawn to the prosthesis where the woman's left foot should be, but she dragged her eyes back up to meet the dark ones looking at her with sympathy.

"*Somebody start talking,*" she grated, glaring at the others and trying to pull her shit together. "Where's my husband? *What's going on?*"

"Your husband is safe," the black woman said quickly, a pleasant Caribbean accent coloring her words. "Our friend is transporting him back to the pyramid complex. It's a much faster method of travel than walking would be."

Amy pressed the heel of her hand into her eye socket, remembering a confused sense of being whisked through the air, out of the excavation pit — her surroundings a formless blur.

"This is insane," she whispered.

The man and the woman exchanged a glance, as though they were somehow conversing silently.

The woman met Amy's eyes again, giving her a smile that was doubtless meant to be reassuring. "It's all a bit complicated, I'm afraid. Right now, we should probably concentrate on getting you back to safety." She indicated the man. "This is Chan Wei Yong. He and the wolves are going to look after you. With this foot of mine, I'd only slow you down walking on sand. It makes more sense for me to do aerial surveillance and make certain nothing nasty is waiting for us between here and there."

"Aerial surveillance?" Amy echoed weakly.

"That's right." The woman smiled again. She truly was lovely, and something in Amy wanted to trust her as she continued, "Chan, have you got this?"

"We're good," Chan said curtly. "Go ahead. We'll stay here until you circle back and give the all-clear."

"Okay," said the woman, looking at Amy again. "Now, don't be afraid…"

With no more warning than that, her slender body warped and changed, reality twisting until a small brown owl with white flecks on its wings stood balanced on one leg in the sand where she had been an instant before.

Amy stared at the bird, her mouth hanging open and her eyes as wide as dinner plates. She watched as the dark owl flapped its wings, launched itself upward, and took off into the dark sky above her head.

"*Oh...* wow." Amy saw the bird swoop ahead of them, scouting for danger. Her mind had gone suddenly numb, as though it was pretty much done with the whole 'accepting input from her senses' thing today. "Yeah, okay. I think I'm really losing it this time." She reached for her ponytail, pulled it out, and ran shaky fingers through her tangled hair.

So... *yeah.*

Experiencing a psychotic break was quite a bit different than how she'd imagined it would be, she mused. It was a lot trippier, for one thing. Because... owls? *Seriously?*

It wasn't just owls, though. She frowned at the huge canines standing guard nearby. "Are those werewolves?" she asked Chan matter-of-factly.

"Sort of," Chan said.

She nodded. "Right. The, uh... the vampire guy back at the compound said not to get him started on werewolves or zombies. I guess I can see why now."

"Xander, you mean?" Chan pointed to one of the great beasts. "That's him, actually. Technically, he's a vampire who got bitten by a werewolf."

The other wolf growled.

"Oops, sorry." Chan moved his pointing finger. "*That's* him. I have kind of a hard time telling them apart until he growls at me. The other one is Manisha. She's a werewolf who got bitten by a vampire. Like Oksana said, it's... a bit complicated."

Amy stared at them, feeling a bit dizzy now as her adrenaline started to crash. "Uh-huh. I can see that."

Chan glanced up at the owl, which had circled back to them. "It looks like the way ahead is clear. Let's get you back to your husband."

With those words, Amy's fragile shell of calm shattered, and she wavered on her feet. Chan's hand darted out and steadied her by the upper arm.

"Whoa... you sure you're all right?" he asked.

"No," she said faintly.

He nodded, his features set in an expression of understanding under the silver light of the rising moon. "Okay, that's fair enough. But can you walk?"

"Yes." If it meant she could get to wherever the impossible pharaoh guy had taken Elijah, she'd fucking walk if it killed her.

"Let's go, then." Chan didn't let go of her arm, though his sharp eyes scanned the surroundings as he led her away from the grisly excavation site. "This place won't stay secure forever."

The wolves flanked them, the one on her left walking close enough that its fur brushed her leg occasionally. It was beautiful, with a silver pelt and black-tipped ears. Her free hand landed on the thick fur of its shoulders before she realized she'd reached out to touch. Gold-brown eyes flicked up to meet hers with the same soul-deep sadness Amy had seen in Manisha's on the day they'd arrived in Egypt. She caught her breath, but the animal had already returned to scanning the desert around them for threats.

The stench of rotting corpses still swirled around her. It was in her hair, on her clothes. She tried putting it out of her mind, but that was impossible.

She glanced at Chan, needing distraction. "Are you a vampire too, then?"

"Yes," Chan answered as they continued along the dusty road leading to the compound.

"So, can you turn into an owl?"

"Yes."

"And that weird… vapor thing? Can you do that?"

"Yes."

"In that case, if you're worried about more zombies coming, shouldn't we go back that way instead of walking?"

He shot her an inscrutable look. "Believe me, I would if I could. But apparently Menkhef is the only vampire powerful enough to transport other living beings that way. I can barely manage to keep track of my clothes and small inanimate objects."

"So he's that most powerful vampire. Got it."

She wondered why some of them called him Snag and some of the called him Menkhef. Menkhef certainly sounded like a good name for a vampire that looked like he should have his own pyramid somewhere.

Snag… not so much.

For the remainder of the journey, Amy kept her questions to herself. They spent the next twenty minutes or so trudging through the sandy desert. At least, Amy trudged. Chan strode with graceful, confident strides, and the wolves padded over the sand on silent paws. Amy didn't see much of the owl—just the occasional dark silhouette in the sky ahead of them.

She let out a silent breath of relief when they arrived at the grand entrance to the step pyramid complex. Amy followed Chan as he led her to what Elijah had called the South Tomb. They ascended a set of stone steps leading to the top of the wall studded with stone cobra heads, and then down into the catacombs below.

At first, Amy couldn't help but shiver at the idea of entering that dark world. She was surprised to find LED bulbs strung overhead, pushing back the stifling darkness to reveal intricate carvings and paintings on the walls. If she hadn't been a complete wreck over Elijah and the horror of the last hour, she might have taken a moment to appreciate them. As it was, her thoughts raced in frantic circles. Was Elijah okay? Could she trust these people?

Because… they weren't people. They were vampires, and werewolves, and apparently fucking *zombies* existed and were trying to kill them all. She was still on the fence about the whole 'psychotic break' thing, not least because it was a lot less scary than believing what she'd seen was real.

And then there was the man. The one who had tilted her world on its axis with a handful of silent words, barely more than a day ago. He'd looked straight at her after rescuing them from certain death and called her his heart; then he'd looked at Elijah and called him his soul. What did that mean? His eyes, when he'd said those things...

She shivered again. He'd touched them both, and a jolt of pure power ran through her. She'd never felt anything remotely like it in her life.

"Here we are," Chan said. He stood at the entrance of a chamber and ushered her inside.

It was surprisingly large. She barely had a chance to take in that fact, along with the basic medical setup and the presence of other people, before the figure on the cot in the center of the room grabbed her attention.

"*Elijah!*" She rushed to his side, tears welling up in her eyes.

A sandy-haired man with slate blue eyes stood beside the cot. He was placing an IV needle in Elijah's vein, the flexible plastic tube attached to a hanging bag of fluid.

Red fluid.

"Is that... blood?" Amy tensed, her protective instincts rushing to the fore. "What are you *doing*? He hasn't lost any blood, and you don't even know his blood type!"

The man gave Amy a reassuring look that was wholly ineffective. "In this particular case," he said in a pronounced Australian accent, "the only thing

I need to know about his blood type is that it's human."

He straightened from the IV as red started flowing through the long tube toward Elijah's arm. "I'm Dr. Mason Walker. Your husband suffered a severe head wound, but it just so happens, you're in luck. You happened to be in the same neighborhood as a bunch of vampires."

"What are you *talking about*?" Amy demanded, her muscles tense as she debated whether to spring forward and drag the needle out of her husband's vein.

Just as she decided to do it, the supposed doctor's eyes flared with an inner light, and her brain went foggy.

"Give me a few moments to explain the situation," the doctor said calmly, and Amy felt that calm spread through her as well. "I'm sorry to influence you like this, but I promise it's only for a minute, and only to ensure that your husband gets the care he needs as quickly as possible."

"What's... going on?" she asked, much more reasonably this time. "I don't understand."

"Vampire blood has extraordinary healing properties in humans," the man told her, still in the same soothing voice. "Your husband took a bad blow to the skull and was showing signs of bleeding on the brain. In human medicine, that kind of thing takes some serious medical firepower to treat that I don't have access to out here, but I do have access to something even better."

"Vampire blood?" Amy echoed blankly, feeling on some level like she should be way more freaked out right now than she was.

"That's right," the doctor said. He gestured to a corner, and Amy was surprised to see their rescuer skulking like a shadow, unmoving and silent. "Menkhef here donated a pint for him that will have him as good as new in no time. Look. You'll be able to see as it starts working."

Amy followed his pointing finger and gulped. The side of Elijah's head was a mess of swelling and bruising, his eyes swollen shut and his features on that side practically unrecognizable. A wash of gray encroached on the edges of her vision as she realized that the blow might easily have killed him.

"Easy," the doctor told her, and another wave of calm pushed back on the hysteria. "Look closer."

She swallowed hard and looked closer. As she watched, the swelling seemed to recede, the progress slow but detectable to the naked eye.

"Just give his body a bit of time to repair itself," the blue-eyed man continued. "He'll be fine. My word on it."

SIXTEEN

Elijah struggled to move—to regain awareness of his surroundings and *wake the hell up*. He needed to make sure Amy was all right. Something really, really bad had happened, and then something… else… had happened, and now he couldn't seem to make his brain function, much less the rest of his body.

For a few moments, it had felt like he was moving, a sweeping feeling of vertigo joining the pounding ache in his head and the sense of being stuffed to the gills with cotton wool. Then the dizzy sensation of flying—or maybe falling—subsided. Without even that much feedback from the outside world, he lost his grip on anything resembling consciousness. Between one moment and the next, disorientation became black nothingness—a smooth, untouched canvas to act as the backdrop for strange fever dreams.

-o-o-o-

Heqab looked up as the skinny messenger boy scurried through the confusion of sparring military recruits. His small body darted between the larger, heavily muscled ones raising clouds of dust in the late afternoon light as they clashed in simulated battle. He skidded to a halt in front of Heqab, breathless, his small chest rising and falling rapidly.

"Captain!" the child piped in a high, clear voice. "The nomarch orders that you join him at the palace for a private meeting when the sun touches the trees over the western bank of the Nile!"

Heqab covered a sigh, a flash of irritation furrowing his brow before he smoothed it. He had much to do today, and would have preferred not to waste the last of the precious daylight in some endless strategy meeting with Menkhef that could have been scheduled later in the evening. Sometimes, he felt that the ruler of the Nome of the Northern Sycamore was inclined to take advantage of their boyhood friendship, presuming on his time in a way that he would not have done with an older and more experienced commander.

Or… it might have had more to do with the fact that Heqab folded like a sodden rag to every single such request. His old friend had not ascended to the governorship of a prefecture without being both charismatic and persuasive.

"Very well," he told the boy, resignation coloring his tone. "Tell the nomarch that I will join him at the appointed time."

The messenger nodded, wide-eyed, and hared off again — avoiding the training soldiers as deftly as he'd done on the way in. Heqab's eyes followed him for a few moments, thinking the lad might be useful in the infantry in a few years.

Trying not to let speculation about the subject of the upcoming meeting distract him, he turned his attention back to the task at hand — teaching a dozen raw conscripts how to string a bow without putting their own eyes out during the process. Or putting out anyone else's eyes, for that matter.

Menkhef probably wanted to talk more about the rumblings from the pharaoh's court, whispers that Qahedjet intended to consolidate his power over the dozens of small administrative districts running up and down the length of the Nile. The pharaoh had always been the ultimate ruler in the region—a god made flesh—but in practice, the nomarchs had been seizing more local power for themselves for many years now.

Heqab dragged his focus back to the present just in time to stop one of the would-be archers from using a knot to secure his bowstring that would have slipped loose the first time he tried to nock an arrow. He told himself firmly that he would find out what Menkhef considered so important soon enough.

The afternoon slipped by in a haze of heat and blazing sunlight. At intervals, Heqab shaded his eyes as he gauged the progress of Ra's chariot across the sky. As it approached the western horizon, he wrapped up the day's training and headed off for his summons. He was sweaty and covered in dust, but he decided not to bathe before presenting himself at the palace.

Let that small act of defiance communicate my opinion on having my workday cut short, he thought dryly. It wasn't as though Menkhef would take any great offense over the minor slight from his childhood companion. Frankly, he'd probably find it amusing.

Heqab stalked up to the palace entrance, where he was met by a servant who bowed low and immediately ushered him toward the central courtyard. That was a relief, at least—the day had been a brutally hot one, and the last thing Heqab needed was to be stuck in a stuffy stone room, baking like a clay pot in an oven. The servant indicated the table set in the middle of the shady space, and bowed again before withdrawing.

Heqab followed the direction of the gesture with his eyes. He halted abruptly, surprise and another emotion he didn't care to examine freezing him momentarily in place. Three chairs were ranged around the low table, which was piled high with fruit, bread, meat, and cheese. It wasn't the feast that gave him pause, however; it was the woman seated in front of it with Menkhef.

Nebetta. The nomarch's consort.

The woman Heqab had loved since he was barely old enough to wield a spear.

Menkhef swirled his goblet of wine, drawing Heqab's attention away from dangerous territory. The nomarch raised a tolerant eyebrow, his lips twitching faintly with what might have been amusement.

"I wasn't aware that we had commissioned a new statue for the entrance of the courtyard," he said mildly, still with that faint teasing gleam in his eye.

Heqab felt blood rise to his face, relieved that his dark skin hid the flush. He forced himself forward, cursing his callow reaction to Nebetta's unexpected presence.

"And I wasn't aware that you would be providing enough food for the entire regiment, Your Excellence," he retorted. "I didn't realize I was supposed to invite them along."

The smile tugging at Menkhef's lip grew wider for a moment before he hid it behind the mask of a ruler. Heqab approached the table and stopped a few steps away, bowing at the waist.

"My queen," he said respectfully, all hints of banter gone.

"Captain," she replied in her warm, honeyed voice, making no attempt to hide her pleasure at his presence. "Thank you for coming on such short notice."

"I wouldn't dream of ignoring such a summons," he said immediately.

In truth, Nebetta would not have been considered a queen by most in the Kingdom of Egypt. She was the wife of a nomarch — an administrative governor. While all three of them hailed from noble families, they were hardly royalty in the pharaoh's eyes. In both Menkhef and Heqab's eyes, however, Nebetta was royalty. For Menkhef, it was because he intended to establish his own dynasty with her in the Land of the Northern Sycamore — a dynasty to rival the pharaoh's. For Heqab, it was because she had always ruled his heart from afar.

Many times over the past few years, Heqab had wondered at the fact that his poorly hidden yearning for the nomarch's consort had not resulted in his banishment from the land he called home. As far as he could tell, it hadn't even put strain on the friendship that bound him to his ruler — for all that their friendship was now hidden under the duties of soldier and leader.

Perhaps it was because Heqab had never allowed his behavior to become unseemly. Perhaps it was because he loved Menkhef, too, and Menkhef knew it. As lads, they'd been joined at the hip, close enough in station not to raise eyebrows with their friendship, but both acutely aware of the paths already laid out for their lives.

As soon as Menkhef had reached his majority and attained the position of regional governor, it became clear that Nebetta would be his and not Heqab's. He'd never once rubbed Heqab's face in that knowledge, and in some ways it had been easier to watch her marry someone Heqab cared for so dearly. Especially since Heqab knew that Menkhef loved her with every bit as much passion as he did.

Heqab could not overstate his gratitude toward Menkhef for allowing his unrequited longing to remain in the shadows, unremarked—for bringing it into the open would surely ruin him

"Sit, old friend," Menkhef said, gesturing to the empty seat at the table. Gracious, as always, and with a look in his dark eyes that said he knew something Heqab didn't.

Heqab sat. "Thank you. Now, what did you wish to speak with me about?"

"Eat first," Menkhef insisted, waving a lazy hand at the food. "I may not have the entire army here to deal with this embarrassing amount of food, but that only means I need to make full use of the one soldier I do have."

Heqab flickered an eyebrow that communicated his opinion of being put off in such a way, but he started loading fruit and cheese onto a copper dish without comment. It had been a trying day even if it had also been an abbreviated one, and he hadn't eaten anything since a chunk of unleavened bread dipped in oil late that morning.

Nebetta kept up a stream of pleasant conversation on light subjects as they ate, putting him at ease like she always did. Menkhef was his usual charming but inscrutable self, and before Heqab knew it, his stomach was full, his wine glass was empty, and he was far too sated and relaxed to want to discuss military strategy or — gods forbid — political strategy.

The servant who had shown him in returned with two others to clear away the detritus of the meal. Menkhef halted the young man with a glance and said, "Take the food back to the kitchens and put it away. Then dismiss everyone for the evening, yourself included, Sef. I desire to speak to the captain in private."

"Yes, Your Excellence," the servant said immediately. "I will see to it at once."

Heqab frowned, curiosity rising to war with his pleasant state of drowsiness. The other two continued to chat about nothing for a few more minutes, until Sef returned and bowed to the nomarch.

"The others are leaving now," he said. "I will follow and secure the door on my way out."

"Thank you," Menkhef said calmly, and waited until the sound of fading footsteps disappeared, leaving the building in eerie silence as the light faded into dusk above the courtyard.

Heqab expected Menkhef to ask Nebetta to leave as well, but he made no move to do so. Unease began to war with the curiosity running rife inside his mind. Unable to contain himself any longer, Heqab turned to his ruler. "Forgive me," he said, "but I had assumed you wished to speak about the rumors coming from the pharaoh's court. Was I mistaken?"

Menkhef smiled, but Heqab thought he could detect a hint of tension in the expression. "In a manner of speaking, you are correct," he said cryptically. "We do wish to speak with you about the implications of Qahedjet's power grab, but not in a… military capacity."

The 'we' made Heqab's brow furrow in confusion. As far as he knew, Nebetta had never involved herself in her husband's political machinations. Not in any sort of active role.

"I… don't understand, Your Excellence," he hazarded, looking between them.

Menkhef's eyes flicked to Nebetta for a moment, the small physical manifestation of nervousness doing more to disquiet Heqab than anything that had come before. Menkhef did not display uncertainty. He decided to do something and did it without a second thought. To Heqab's further shock, it was Nebetta who spoke next, rather than her husband.

"Menkhef and I wish to establish a ruling line for this land," she said in her low, decadent voice. "The pharaoh does not know what the land of the

Northern Sycamore needs. Nor does he much care. The people need their own rulers, and without a dynasty in place, there will be too much uncertainty about the future."

Heqab knew this already. He looked between the two of them, feeling like someone had thrown him into the Nile without a rope during the spring floods.

"And… you wish to discuss some aspect of this with me?" he asked.

Nebetta blinked her large eyes. "I have not yet fallen pregnant."

The sense of being buffeted by an unpredictable current grew stronger, and he floundered for any sort of suitable response. "You are young yet, my queen. It signifies nothing—"

"It signifies that after more than five years of marriage, I have been unable to give my queen a child," Menkhef said evenly, and Heqab's attention swung back to him.

It took him even longer to formulate a reply to that. "You… are the nomarch, Menkhef. No one would protest if you took a second wife to bear you children."

He had to force himself not to look back at Nebetta, unsure if she would be hurt by the suggestion. It was true that polygamy wasn't common in Egypt, but it wasn't totally unheard of among the upper classes. In a case like this, it wouldn't raise eyebrows, even though something inside Heqab burned on Nebetta's behalf at the implication that she somehow wasn't good enough.

"It is true," Menkhef agreed, still in that calm, even tone. "No one would protest. However, all of the female members of Nebetta's family old enough to do so have borne several healthy babes in short order, while my mother only ever birthed me... and died while doing so. A second wife will no more be able to provide us with a child than Nebetta has been able to... if the problem lies with me.

Heqab stared at him, dumbfounded. Menkhef blinked at him.

"Have I shocked you?" His voice grew dry. "Your mouth is hanging open in a thoroughly un-appealing manner, Captain."

He snapped it shut, and considered before answering, "Yes. You've shocked me. In twenty-six years of life, I have never heard a man admit that his wife's failure to bear children might be his fault."

Menkhef shrugged. "Then those men are fools. I care nothing for the perceived slight to my man-hood. All that interests me is solving the problem. My wife comes from a family of fertile mother-goddesses, and I come from scorched and barren earth. It seems clear enough."

"But why tell me this?" Heqab asked, at an utter loss as to why he was even here. "In what way can I possibly help with this situation? I'm a *soldier*, Menkhef."

"You love her," Menkhef said simply, and Heqab's thoughts solidified into marble.

A moment later, there was a loud clatter, and he realized he'd leapt to his feet, sending his chair crashing to the ground behind him. He pointed a shaking finger at the nomarch.

"I have never once shown the least impropriety toward our queen, Menkhef," he ground out, anger and mortification flooding him at having his scandalous secret dragged into the open without warning. Why would Menkhef lull him into a sense of security for *years*, only to betray him like this in front of *Nebetta herself*? "I have never wavered in my loyalty to you—not *once*! Yet you would bring me here to… *what*? Accuse me?"

"Husband." Nebetta's soft voice cut through Heqab's distress. "You are making a terrible mess of this."

Heqab's frantic gaze flew to her, his chest heaving as wildly as the little messenger boy's had been earlier. He had a terrible feeling that his emotions were as clear in his eyes as if a scribe had inked them on papyrus for the world to see.

"Why did you call me here?" he whispered, not even sure which one of them he was addressing anymore.

"You love Nebetta," Menkhef said again, still infuriatingly calm. "You also love me. Your allegiance has never been in question, old friend. We have watched for years as you put aside your feelings in the name of duty and loyalty. And for that, we love you back with equal ferocity."

Heqab fumbled behind him for the overturned chair and righted it so that he could half-fall into it. *"I don't understand what you're saying to me."*

Nebetta rose, graceful and regal as always, circling the table to stand next to him. She took his right hand in both of hers and lifted it to her cheek. "Before my beloved Menkhef is forced to take a second wife, I would have you as a second husband."

Heqab looked up at her with a lifetime's worth of longing, his palm burning where it touched the smooth silk of her flawless golden skin.

"It doesn't work that way," he whispered hoarsely.

"I cannot offer you public acknowledgement," Menkhef said quietly. He hadn't moved, but his eyes watched them both with aching fondness. "I cannot offer you true fatherhood in the eyes of the people, should Nebetta bear children. But, on my life, I swear that should you accept our plea and join us in our bed, you will always be welcome there. I will name you my family's personal guard rather than my army's captain, and you will have access to your children day and night as their protector."

Something caught in Heqab's chest, a choked noise emerging as he pictured children with Nebetta's beautiful eyes laughing and shrieking with joy as he taught them to shoot a bow and arrow or hunt with a spear.

"I..." he began unsteadily. "I don't..."

His hand was shaking where it rested against Nebetta's cheek, and so was the rest of him. Menkhef rose smoothly from his chair, approaching him from the other side.

"Don't make your choice tonight. Give us your answer only when you are ready, old friend," he said.

A hand closed around the back of Heqab's neck, and Menkhef pulled him into an embrace. Heqab felt himself caught between the two them. Held there, wordless, his heart lurching wildly inside his chest.

"Know that you are the only one I would ever trust with this, Heqab," Menkhef continued. "The only one I would ever ask. We don't seek this solution at any price. Only at your pleasure."

-o-o-o-

Much later, Heqab lay alone in his hut on his straw-stuffed sleeping pad, staring into the darkness at the thatched roof above him. Menkhef had told him not to make his choice tonight, but in reality, there was no choice at all. His oldest friend had just asked him to claim the woman he'd loved as long as he could remember, and give her children to rule a kingdom.

What answer could there possibly be, besides *yes*?

SEVENTEEN

"**I** don't care if the bruising is going down! This is still *completely fucking insane*! He *needs* to get a CT scan, and he needs to be seen by specialists!"

Elijah winced as the outside world intruded on his dreams, Amy's shrill and slightly hysterical sounding words jolting him back to the present.

"He really doesn't, you know," said an unfamiliar male voice.

Wait. That was weird. What the hell was Hugh Jackman doing here?

He tried to pry sticky eyelids apart, but it was as though he'd forgotten how. It felt like there were a whole lot of things he should be worrying about... but, as ever, when Amy was upset, everything else faded to unimportance.

"Ames?" he croaked, finally managing to peel one eyelid open.

All sound in the area ceased, and then Amy cried, "*Elijah!*" and practically flung herself into his arms. He lay flat on his back, holding her against his chest as she sobbed, and tried to remember how to make his brain cells work.

"Are you all right?" she choked out after a few moments. "Are you in pain?"

He paused, taking stock. A hazy vision of a creature from his darkest nightmares swinging a heavy wooden board at his head flickered before his eyes... a sound, dull, but deafening as it connected, and then, confusion.

Elijah lifted a hand from Amy's shoulders to gingerly prod at the side of his skull. The skin felt faintly tender and stretched, like an old bruise, nearly healed. "Not... really?" he hazarded, because while it didn't in fact hurt, something told him it really, really should have.

"Give it another few minutes, mate," said Hugh Jackman. "You'll be good as new, promise."

He blinked, managing to get both eyes working this time. He was on a cot in a dimly lit room with stone walls. It was cool, but the atmosphere was stuffy in a way that was familiar from his days working in subterranean dig sites.

"Are we underground?" he asked, more memories starting to trickle in.

"Yes," Amy said, her voice more controlled and less terrified now. "We're under the... South Tomb? Is that right?"

"That's correct," Hugh Jackman confirmed.

Elijah dragged his eyes from Amy to the source of the Australian accent. Not Hugh Jackman after all, but a well-built, sandy-haired man with blue eyes and a professional demeanor. "What happened?" he asked. "How did we get here?"

"What's the last thing you remember?" the Aussie asked.

Elijah frowned, and couldn't even feel the bruising on his head this time. "There was... a courtyard, and... a table, piled high with food. Menkhef wanted to see me—"

A sharp indrawn breath came from the shadows at the back of the room, out of Elijah's line of sight.

Amy's brows drew together in worry. "Elijah? What are you talking about?"

He blinked, the memory sliding away as more pressing images crowded in. Saqqara. The Imhotep Museum. The group in the village. The Headless Pyramid—

"The zombies. Holy shit. Amy, are you all right?" His eyes flew to her, searching for injuries.

"I think it's coming back to him now," said a dry British voice. He recognized the man who'd spoken to them when they left the compound. lounging by the doorway with his arms crossed. The Indian woman, Manisha, stood next to him, watching Elijah with interest.

"I'm okay," Amy reassured. "Just a few scrapes and a wrenched shoulder."

"Manisha. Xander," said the Australian. "Go let the others know he's awake, and that everyone needs to bugger off for a bit."

"Come on, love," said the Englishman. "It appears our presence is surplus to requirements."

"We'll let them know, Mason," Manisha said.

When they were gone, the Australian gestured Amy back so that he could get at Elijah's arm. Elijah hadn't even noticed the I.V., he'd been so wrapped up in what was going on around him. It led to an empty bag hanging nearby, traces of red visible inside.

"Is that a blood transfusion?" he asked, wondering how badly he'd been hurt. Surely it couldn't have been too awful since he felt pretty darned good right now, all things considered.

"It's a *vampire* blood transfusion," Amy said tightly, and pressed her lips together in an unhappy line.

Unease trickled down Elijah's spine. "*Excuse me?*"

"From what I understand, you were unconscious for most of the interesting parts of Chan and Oksana's explanations," the man name Mason observed mildly. "But, yes, we're vampires. I'm also a doctor, as it happens, and I gave you a pint of Menkhef's blood to heal you. You suffered serious head trauma and it was the safest way of ensuring there was no permanent damage. Vampire blood is basically a miracle cure for humans."

Menkhef. There was that name again.

But he needed to prioritize. There were too many crazy assertions being thrown around, and while his head might not be spinning from a concussion, it was whirling nonetheless. "Amy...?"

Amy perched on the edge of his cot. "I don't know what to tell you, Elijah. You remember the zombies. Do you remember the wolves showing up?"

Her words brought images in their wake, and feelings, too. The sudden realization that what he had thought was reality was only a comforting illusion. The absolute fear upon realizing that Amy's life was in danger and he wasn't strong enough to protect her.

"*I told you to run,*" he accused in a hoarse tone.

She shrugged and took his hand between both of hers. "Yeah, sorry. That was never going to happen. Not unless you ran with me." She cleared her throat, trying to bring her emotions under control. "Anyway, the wolves showed up and started tearing into those... *things*... attacking us. A few minutes later, three more people appeared and joined the fight. They say they're vampires, and I believe them, Elijah. The things I saw—"

"Amy," he said softly.

She shook her head. "One of the creatures hit you, and you tumbled into an open excavation shaft. The man—the one we met that first night— he rescued you and flew you to safety somehow. Then he came back for me. The vampires fought off the zombie things, and he flew you to safety while the rest of us followed on foot."

Elijah squeezed her fingers as she cradled his hand in hers. "As long as you're safe."

She squeezed back. "Your head... that thing hit you so hard. I was afraid you'd die." Her voice quavered, and she swallowed hard, steadying it. "They said their blood could heal you, and almost as soon as the IV was attached, the swelling started to go down. I tried to argue that you still needed proper medical care... and then you woke up. You're sure you're okay now?"

It was... one hell of a story. But to discount it completely would be to call Amy a liar, and Amy *wasn't* a liar. He touched his head again with his free hand. It felt completely normal now. With a deep breath, Elijah swung carefully into a sitting position, not releasing his grip on Amy.

"Yeah," he said, in some surprise. "I actually feel… fine. A bit thirsty, I guess."

"Not for blood, I hope?" Amy joked weakly.

The Australian chuckled. "It doesn't really work that way. To become a vampire, you have to be drained to the edge of death before drinking vampire blood. That's…" His eyes slid to the shadows at the back of the room. "… a conversation for another time."

Both Elijah and Amy followed his gaze in time to see a tall figure step into the light. Elijah's breath caught, dream images once more blurring with reality as that face from the distant past emerged into view. He couldn't look away, even when the doctor spoke again.

"You should be fine now," he said, "but I'd still like you to take it easy for a few hours. Get something to eat and drink. I'd tell you to sleep, but… I'm afraid that may not be in the cards for any of us. I'll leave you to speak with Menkhef, but if you need me, he can call for me, or you can. Just give a yell. I'll be nearby."

The doctor tidied the medical equipment out of the way and paused, shooting the mysterious figure in the corner what looked like a significant glance before leaving the three of them alone. Silence reigned for several moments as Elijah tried to reconcile the conflicting images whirling inside his mind.

Menkhef, brushing a strand of Amy's hair back as he told them not to let the Darkness steal away their Light.

Menkhef, rising from the remains of an ancient Egyptian feast to embrace him like a brother after granting him his fondest wish.

Menkhef, leaning over him in the desert, his worried face blurring beneath the dizzying pain of a concussion.

Menkhef, reclining on a carved wooden divan in an ancient courtyard, his head thrown back in ecstasy as the woman they both loved writhed between them, crying out as she came.

Elijah's heart kicked hard, like a surprised mule driving its heels repeatedly into his chest. Beside him, Amy stiffened. Her green eyes narrowed, pinning the man who now haunted both Elijah's dreams and his waking world.

"Explain," she demanded, nearly spitting the word. "*Explain all of this to us.*"

Menkhef did not move closer; he merely inclined his head, his chin rising.

"I will," he promised. "And I am sorry for what you will learn."

EIGHTEEN

Amy gripped Elijah's hand like a lifeline, glaring at the vampire who had saved them only to disappear into the shadows immediately afterward without a word of explanation. She didn't know why she was suddenly so angry — at herself, at the vampires running this place, at Shay and her cheerful acceptance of the madness around them…

At Elijah, for trying to convince her to leave him behind during the attack. At the world, for not making sense. Okay, maybe she did know why she was angry. But, *by god*, she was finished with this shit. She was getting answers, and she was damned well getting them *now*.

"Explain," she spat. *"Explain all of this to us."*

Elijah was frozen next to her, though she could feel his pulse galloping. The vampire barely moved, only regarding them with dark eyes.

"I will," he promised. "And I am sorry for what you will learn."

He was so… damned… *beautiful*, standing there like some ancient work of art, and it only made her angrier. How dare he look so fucking tragic as he was promising to explain things, like he knew the story they'd been thrust into wouldn't have a happy ending. She opened her mouth to snap, *Stop apologizing and start making sense!* —

And then a freight train slammed into her thoughts and steamrolled her into the ground.

A confused tangle of images and feelings plowed into her consciousness in no particular order. *So many.* Far too many to belong to a single person. Far too many to fit inside her brain at once. Her skull would crack under the pressure any second now, four thousand years of history spilling onto the dusty stone floor…

The pressure eased, another mind surrounding hers—helping her sort through the swirling tornado of memories and drag them into some kind of coherent narrative.

She was inside Menkhef's memories. The tornado was his life, unfolding before her. She watched him grow up in an ancient land, loving Heqab as a brother and falling in love with Nebetta. *Me*, she thought. *That's me! I remember those dreams… I remember this place! Heqab… Elijah… I remember you now!*

She watched as Menkhef married Nebetta. Watched him mourn their lack of children as the years went by. Until one day, he made a suggestion and Nebetta's eyes lit up with hope, her overflowing love nearly spilling from her skin, it was so radiant. Soon after, they had Heqab with them, and Nebetta bore her two lovers a girl and a boy—perfect and beautiful and *theirs*.

For more than ten years, Menkhef lived a life far better than any mortal deserved, watching his family grow and his land prosper. Until one day, a dark evil descended on the palace and turned him into a ravening monster. He killed Nebetta and when her blood wasn't enough, he killed Heqab, too. It still wasn't enough, but the priests and the warriors came, casting spells and tangling him in heavy fishing nets until he was too weakened and injured to get free.

Then, the priests ordered him dragged before his hated enemy, the Pharaoh Qahedjet, and turned him over as a gift to prevent war. Qahedjet kept him in a stone cell and forced him to fight animals in the arena. Despite the burning thirst for blood, he refused to drink from humans, surviving on animal blood until even that comfort was taken away. Eventually, too weakened from starvation to heal from his injuries, he fell into a coma and Qahedjet had him entombed below Djoser's pyramid.

The millennia that followed were slow torture... until one day, the sound of tools chipping away at stone gave way to a shaft of dusty torchlight and the first breath of fresh air to enter the small chamber since the pharaoh's stonemasons had sealed it.

There you are, came a pleasant voice, echoing in their thoughts. *I thought I heard you whispering to me. Looks like I'm not alone after all... though I'll confess I feel a bit odd talking to a petrified mummy. Let me figure out how to get you out of this place, and we'll go from there.*

The grave robber's name was Eris, and he had the patience of Osiris. After decades of drinking Eris' blood a few drops at a time, Amy watched Menkhef grow strong enough to finally rise from his bier... though he was not precisely sane. Happily, Eris did not seem particularly bothered by the fact that he was mad, and the centuries passed much more quickly with company.

Especially once chess was invented.

More time passed, and they found other creatures like themselves—all damaged and bleeding inside, cursed to replenish themselves by making the humans bleed in turn. Still, Menkhef refused to feed from any but Eris, and even then, only seldom. Eris shared his blood willingly enough, but Menkhef knew he became complicit in Eris' need to hunt humans, each and every time he drank from him.

The others were obsessed with discovering why the Darkness had raped them and left them cursed to exist in a shadowy half-life. Eventually, Eris discovered an ancient prophecy regarding a council composed of thirteen of the demon Bael's greatest failures that would rise up to defeat him. They waited and watched, but no more vampires appeared, and together they were only six, not thirteen.

Still, Menkhef refused to feed more than was absolutely necessary, but even on the verge of constant starvation, his powers grew year by year. Eventually, the vampires found Della—the reincarnation of the woman who had sacrificed herself to save one of their number from Bael's damnation.

And Menkhef alone realized what the Council of Thirteen represented. Six vampires. Seven reincarnated mates. The key to holding back the wave of Darkness threatening to eat the world.

But only if they were strong enough to step into the Light.

-o-o-o-

The tidal wave of memories subsided, and Amy's knees gave out. She crumpled to the floor, tears streaming from her eyes, vaguely aware that Elijah had followed her down, his hand still linked with hers.

"It can't be true," she whispered.

The man she'd loved almost five thousand years ago moved to crouch silently next to her, forming the third point of a triangle with the man she'd loved since she was twenty-one. His dark eyes shone with pinpricks of molten bronze. Beside her, Elijah shifted his grip on her hand, lacing their fingers together. With his other hand, he reached out and gripped the vampire's upper arm.

"It's true, Amy," he said, sounding like something inside him had cracked open, spilling out its contents. His gaze moved to Menkhef's and held. "I remember you. *Jesus Christ.* I *dreamed* you. I dreamed… this."

The vampire lifted a long-fingered hand, hovering an inch above Amy's skin for a moment before lowering it to rest lightly on her forearm. Electricity thrummed between them, raising every tiny hair on Amy's body and pulling a gasp free from her lips.

She jerked away from both of them, scuttling backward until her shoulders hit the sandstone wall behind her. "Oh my god. Oh my god, *oh my god.* I can't do this. It's too much—"

Elijah's hand fell from the vampire's arm. He looked nearly as shell-shocked as she felt.

I would not ask it of you on my own behalf. The mental voice was calm. Composed and deep, but sad beyond measure. *I am not the same person I was then, and neither are you. If neither one of you wished to grace my presence ever again, I would understand.* His chest rose and fell. *But that does not negate the responsibility we hold as the final battle for humanity draws near. Bael is coming for the world, and the Council is the only thing standing in the way of the oncoming Darkness.*

She swallowed, her dry throat clicking. "But… we're here. All thirteen. Right? Isn't that what you supposedly need?"

His look of sadness grew deeper, but to her surprise, it was Elijah who spoke.

"The others are all vampires."

A strange kind of panic gripped Amy by the throat. The last couple of days had been so… surreal. People turning into owls, or wolves, or mist. Teenagers with needle tracks on their arms from giving blood donations to vampires. Zombies overrunning an innocent town full of people. Elijah's life-threatening head wound, healing right before her eyes in a handful of minutes.

But there was something more real and immediate than any of those things. Something more important than the craziness swirling around them, threatening to drag them under.

"I can't do this. I'm pregnant," she said, wrapping an arm around her belly.

"I know," Menkhef said aloud. "That is why I said I was sorry."

Elijah climbed to his feet slowly, and the vampire rose to match him.

"I don't understand," Elijah said, in a tone that made it clear he expected Menkhef to make him understand pretty damned fast.

One of our number was with child when Bael attacked and turned her, centuries ago, he said in their minds. *The child... did not survive her turning. While the circumstances are different, I cannot guarantee that the results would not be the same.*

Amy made a small noise in the back of her throat and wrapped her other arm around her middle, holding her belly. Elijah seemed to grow three inches taller. He squared up to Menkhef, his hands clenching into fists at his sides.

"Get out," he growled. "*Now.*"

Menkhef only bowed his head in acknowledgement, his body dissolving into vapor before their eyes and swirling away. Elijah whirled and met Amy's eyes, his own expression devastated as Amy's body began to tremble. She curled up against the wall and hugged her midsection harder.

NINETEEN

The last thing Menkhef wanted to do right now was speak with the others. Unfortunately, circumstances were arrayed against his personal preferences in the matter. Ancient and broken he might be, but he was not so broken that he would allow his selfish desire to withdraw into himself to further endanger those under his protection.

His fellow vampires were waiting for him in the largest gallery of the underground tunnel system, where those with well-developed mental powers were still attempting to spread calm and spiritual light over the complex. He materialized silently, steeling himself to face them.

Tré had been seated facing Della, his hand on her face as he borrowed her young, untempered power to bolster his own telepathic abilities. Upon Menkhef's arrival, he lowered his fingers from her temple and opened his eyes. Serious silver-gray met and held Menkhef's gaze. The others recalled at least part of their attention to their surroundings—and the imminent confrontation brewing.

"The undead are massing around us," Tré said. "We may have very little time left. If we are to have any chance to save the humans, we need to complete the Council before it's too late. You must turn them now, Menkhef."

"No," Menkhef said simply.

Tré rose to his feet. "There's more at stake than your feelings on the matter, or theirs. I'm sorry, but if you won't do it, I will."

Menkhef let the others' thoughts filter into his mind through the bond. Della, Trynn, and Manisha were troubled by Tré's words. Chan seemed unsurprised. Oksana, Mason, Xander, and Duchess were shielding heavily. From Eris, he felt compassion, but no sense of whether the second most powerful vampire would support Tré's position or oppose it.

"No," Menkhef repeated mildly. "You will not turn them without their permission. I will not allow it."

Xander rose to stand next to Tré. "I know what you're thinking, Snag," he said. "We can't play the good guys while we're acting like the monsters. I *do* understand—truly. But you must also be aware that we're both out of time and out of options. The final two members of the Council are right down the hall. Will you stand by while Bael's forces crush every person in every one of our enclaves around the globe, when the possible means to stop him is waiting mere meters away?"

"The woman, Amy, is pregnant," Menkhef said, in lieu of a direct answer.

Duchess swore on a sharp breath and surged to her feet. Oksana made a noise of pain, and Xander closed his eyes, chin dipping sharply as though he'd been struck. Tré's silent resolve wavered only for an instant before steadying, but it was now laced with heavy regret.

To Menkhef's surprise, it was Mason who recovered first. "I'll talk to her. Do you know how far along she is?"

"Two months, or perhaps three."

Duchess hugged herself. "I'm coming, too. Tré, if you try to act before we have a chance to speak with her, I'll side with Snag against you."

She was still shielding strongly, her words tight and flat. Menkhef thought she would seek to dissuade Amy from risking her child, but he made himself let go of his fears and expectations regarding what might happen in the coming hours. It was suddenly a far more difficult thing to do than it had been in the weeks since he'd come to the conclusion that the Angel Israfael was influencing things as the final battle approached.

Apparently, it wasn't so easy to trust in Her power when the lives of those he cherished hung in the balance.

"Go," he told Duchess and Mason. "I will remain here. My presence would only complicate matters further."

Duchess raised a sharp brow at Tré, who paused before giving a minute nod of acquiescence. Once the pair had left, Menkhef turned his back on the others and settled into a seated position on the stone floor, intending to once more lend his mental aid in calming and protecting the people above them.

In almost five thousand years of living, clearing his mind of worry for his mates was one of the hardest things he had ever done.

-o-o-o-

Elijah held Amy tightly against his chest. Panic was still thrumming through his veins like ice water. In the space of an hour, his world had been turned upside down; his rational beliefs upended and set on fire. But one thing remained the same as it always had—in the end, Amy and the child she was carrying were the only things that truly mattered to him. He'd failed to protect them at the Headless Pyramid. They would have died if…

He gritted his teeth. It was still almost physically painful to say the word, or even to think it.

Amy and their baby would have died if the *vampires* hadn't shown up and saved them.

But no matter what the cost, Elijah would protect them now. God help him, he just had to figure out how to do it first. How did you protect someone during an apocalypse?

"We could make a run for it," he said against Amy's hair.

"Where would we run?" she croaked. "Elijah… Saqqara is overrun with the living dead, and a demon is coming to take over the world."

He wanted so badly to be able to say, *don't be ridiculous*. But they'd both seen the truth of it; relived it in gory detail. Felt the burn of bitter, acrid black fog and the agony of Menkhef's soul being ripped in two. Maybe Elijah should have scoffed anyway. Dismissed what they'd experienced as a hallucination or some kind of bizarre brainwashing. But he couldn't do it. The truth was wound through the depths of his soul like the roots of an ancient tree. He swallowed hard, a question burning in his chest.

"Did you dream about him, too, Amy?" he asked. "Did you dream about the past—about the three of us together in Egypt?"

She stilled in the circle of his arms. "I dreamed. But it was always hazy. I couldn't recall the details afterward." They were both silent for the space of several breaths before she spoke again. "Is… that why you told me last year that you thought we should see other people? Because of the dreams?"

He stiffened, but she tightened her grip on him, keeping him from pulling away.

"Elijah. Is that why?" she pressed.

His heart was pounding, pride and humiliation urging him to put her off. To keep his secret. But how would keeping his secret help them now? They could well be about to die, overrun by monsters or destroyed by a vengeful demon. Did he really want to go out perpetuating a lie with the woman he loved—even a lie of omission?

"Yes," he said quietly. "I dreamed of you in his arms. And I should have hated it. I should have been enraged by it… but I wasn't. I was… relieved. I loved seeing you with him, and you were so *happy.*"

She was holding onto him so tightly he thought she might leave bruises as she said, "When I dreamed, I couldn't remember much. But sometimes I remembered that I'd been dreaming about loving two men at once. Two men who both loved me, and who cared about each other as well. When I woke up from those dreams, I felt like the luckiest woman on earth." Her chest hitched. "I told myself it was just a stupid sex fantasy. I didn't want to say anything to you about it. I knew you already felt like you weren't enough for me."

"We're both idiots," he murmured into her hair.

She nodded. "I need you to know, Elijah—I never had any desire to start sleeping around or to find another man. It's just, in the dreams, it felt like we were finally…"

"Complete?" he finished.

She paused, mulling the word over. "Yeah. Yeah, that's it. It's like we fit together—the three of us. Stronger with each other to lean on than we ever could have been apart."

"Jesus, Ames," he whispered, cradling her close. "I just hope we have a chance to figure all this out."

A light knock on the door had them breaking apart, the realities around them returning with a vengeance. It creaked open a moment later to admit the Australian doctor and a pale, beautiful blonde woman with a haunted expression lurking behind her china-blue eyes.

"May we come in?" the doctor asked.

Amy hastily scrubbed her palm across her cheeks, as if that would somehow hide the evidence of her tears. "Yes," she said, and glanced at the empty hallway behind them. "Where's—?"

"Menkhef seemed to think his presence might be a distraction," the guy replied. "This is Duchess. She was eight months pregnant when the demon Bael turned her, several hundred years ago. She wanted to speak with you both."

Shit. She must be the one he'd spoken about. No wonder she looked so haunted.

"Okay," Amy managed, her hand creeping to her belly.

"So, talk. Menkhef said turning into a vampire might kill our baby," Elijah said, focusing his attention on the blonde woman. "That means it's not happening. If any of you try to get to her, you'll have to go through me first."

Even as the words passed his lips, new panic rushed through his veins like ice water. He recognized the sheer impotence of the threat. These people could transform themselves into other forms; they had fought off undead creatures that Elijah had been completely powerless against. If they turned on him and Amy, he didn't see any way the two of them could possibly save themselves, and that knowledge ate at him.

"It's true," Duchess, the female vampire, said in a rich French accent. "I miscarried my daughter after the demon attacked me."

The doctor looked between Elijah and Amy, his expression serious. "I want to give you some additional context, here," he said. "This demon wasn't trying to turn Duchess into a vampire. He was trying to turn her into an undead puppet by ripping out half of her soul and destroying it. To aid in that, he thought nothing of destroying her body in the process."

Next to him, Amy shivered, and Elijah thought he saw an answering shudder go through Duchess as well.

"What Bael did to the original vampires in his quest to bend them to his will was brutal beyond all telling," the doctor continued. "No late-term fetus could have been expected to survive that kind of traumatic injury. I want to make it very, very clear that being turned by another vampire is a completely different thing, and I can tell you that from personal experience."

Elijah snaked an arm around Amy's shoulders and held her close against his side, still watching the pair warily.

The doctor sighed. "I can't say it wasn't a traumatic process, though in my case I was already dying—so my experience wasn't exactly typical. But at its most basic, with a healthy human, it involves being drained of blood almost—but not quite—to the point of death. After which, ingesting vampire blood in turn triggers the change."

"What are you getting at?" Elijah demanded. "Because I already made it very clear that the answer is *no*."

"What I'm getting at is this. As a medical professional, nothing about the process is necessarily fatal to a first trimester embryo. The female body goes to surprising lengths to protect the contents of the womb during sudden physiological shocks, and this particular shock need only last a few moments. I'm not convinced that being turned by a powerful vampire who was going to purposeful lengths to make the process as gentle as possible would necessarily cause a miscarriage."

"But it might," Amy said flatly.

"Yes," Duchess replied. "It might."

"It might. But from what I've seen," the doctor said, "Menkhef would expend the last iota of his power to make sure it didn't. And he's the most powerful vampire there is, by quite a large margin."

Elijah's arm tightened around Amy's shoulders, and his voice was hard. "For a doctor, you seem to have a definite bias in this discussion. Shouldn't you be counseling against a procedure that obviously has serious risks, instead of going to such lengths to downplay those risks?"

Up until now, the Australian had remained an affable figure, soft-spoken and calm. But at Elijah's words, his face and tone went stony, while his eyes flared with an inner glow like sunlight on gunmetal.

"I'm going to be blunt, here, Dr. Carpenter—because frankly, we don't have time to beat around the bush," he said. "I've spent my adult life volunteering pediatric medical services in war zones because I care about saving kids. At this moment in time, my brother and his family are running an enclave similar to this one in Singapore. He has two daughters. They're three and five years old. And right now, they are surrounded by an army of walking corpses massing in readiness to attack them—just like the army of walking corpses massing around this compound as we speak."

Elijah's stomach turned over, but he didn't allow it to show on his face as the man continued.

"You two saw those creatures up close. I want you to stop and think very carefully about what they could do to a young child. What they will do to *my nieces* if we don't find a way to stop their attack." A muscle ticked in his square jaw. "I'm sorry that you are forced to face the possibility of losing your unborn child. But your child is not inherently more important than my brother's children, or any of the other untold millions of children who will become prey to Bael's Darkness if we can't stop him, right here and now. Tell me, how long do you think your unborn child will survive when those zombie creatures overrun us?"

Amy was crying again, soft sobs hitching her chest where it pressed against his side.

"*Docteur*," Duchess interrupted softly. "That's enough."

The Australian's flashing eyes turned to her. "You know I'm right about this, Duchess. It's a chance for survival for all of us—this unborn child included—versus no chance at all. Tré knows it. Oksana and Eris know it. Menkhef seems to be the only one who doesn't see it that way."

"He sees more than any of us, I suspect," said the blonde vampire, very softly.

An idea started percolating through the layers of Elijah's mind as the pair spoke. It was still half-formed—terrifying in both its simplicity and its uncertainty.

"I want to talk to Menkhef," he said, before he could second-guess himself. "Get him in here now."

Amy lifted startled eyes to his, a question in her face. Tear tracks left pale streaks through the dust that still dirtied her face after the horror they'd experienced at the Headless Pyramid. He set his jaw, trying to ready himself for what he was about to do.

Duchess' eyes grew distant for a moment before meeting his again. "He's coming."

Elijah swallowed against the dryness of his throat. If the vampires decided to turn on them, as a human, he could do nothing to protect Amy. They were far too strong for him to resist. But if he were a vampire himself...

Menkhef slipped silently into the room, his countless centuries of age showing clearly in the set of his shoulders and the lines around his eyes.

"Turn me," Elijah said, before he could lose his nerve.

Amy gasped and whirled on him. Menkhef raised an eyebrow.

"I won't let you turn Amy," he continued quickly. "But... maybe twelve vampires will be enough for your Council. And... well, if it's not enough, once we see that turning into a vampire is truly safe, then we might reconsider things."

That last part was a lie, but if it sweetened the deal enough to convince Menkhef to turn him first—to make him strong enough to protect her— then his conscience could go to hell. He just wished that Menkhef would stop looking at him with such a depthless expression. An expression that said he knew Elijah better than Elijah knew himself, and that he could see right through him.

"Elijah, no!" Amy exclaimed, grabbing his bicep. Her grip was so tight that her fingernails pricked at his skin, leaving little half-moon indentations in his flesh.

"Ames," he said, meeting her eyes. "Please… just this once, you *have* to trust me."

She opened her mouth as if to argue more, but the words seemed to get caught in her throat. Nothing emerged. He grabbed her free hand and pressed it to the side of his head… the place that had been bruised and shattered before being miraculously healed with vampire blood.

"Think, Amy," he said. "I'll be safer as a vampire than I ever was as a human. I can protect you better that way, from whatever comes next. You, and our baby."

Amy bit her lower lip, chewing at it until he feared she might draw blood.

Very well. Come to me, Menkhef said inside Elijah's mind, still giving him a look that said he knew exactly what Elijah intended, but would give him what he asked for regardless.

Elijah took a step toward him, only to find Amy still clinging to him, her feet set and unmoving. "Amy…" he began.

Menkhef swept the other two vampires with a look. "Leave us," he said softly.

They left, though Duchess paused in the doorway, sending a last, troubled look over her shoulder at Amy. When they were alone, Menkhef turned back to them.

I will not allow the others to change either of you against your will, he said silently, before his gaze narrowed to Elijah alone. *Do you still wish to proceed?*

The words gave him pause, but only for an instant. They were telling in many ways. Elijah even believed them. But it changed nothing. Whether he was protecting Amy from the other vampires or from the undead, he could do it better as a vampire himself.

"Yes," he said, and Amy made a pained noise of denial that pierced his heart like an arrow.

Menkhef approached her and cupped her tear-stained cheek tenderly. "*Hayati*. My heart. Will you trust the two of us to try to keep you safe? You, and the life you carry inside?"

And just like that, Menkhef became complicit in Elijah's plan to protect Amy, rather than being an adversary. The change was so natural and seamless that Elijah might have missed it if not for the way something settled into place inside his chest, the world reorganizing around him until everything made sense for perhaps the first time in his entire damned life.

"He won't hurt me, Ames," Elijah said. "You know he won't."

Menkhef closed his eyes briefly before meeting Elijah's. "Would that it were true, my brave guardsman. I *will* hurt you, though. I will rend your spirit until it tears down the middle, even though it pains me as if it were my own spirit. I can only promise that you will emerge stronger and more powerful on the other side, just as you desire."

Amy stepped away from Menkhef's touch and pressed a hand over her mouth, her body trembling.

"Do it," Elijah said.

As you wish. A heartbeat later, strong hands turned him until Menkhef was standing with his chest to Elijah's back. Power sparked along his nerves at the touch of Menkhef's hands, distracting him as his head was eased to one side. Fangs sunk into the tender skin of his bared throat, and the world whited out around him, descending into flame.

TWENTY

Amy didn't think she'd ever cried so much in her damned life... or been so scared. The feeling of helplessness was the worst thing she'd ever experienced. She couldn't save Elijah, she couldn't save herself, and no matter what decision she made in the end, she might not be able to save her baby.

A wife and mother's worst nightmare, tied up with a neat black bow and placed on a silver platter.

Trust me, Elijah had said, his dark eyes burning into hers with more intensity than she'd ever seen in him. But how could she trust anything or anyone when her husband was writhing in obvious agony, his lips open in a silent scream. She wanted to leap forward and try to wrestle him out of Menkhef's arms, but what if the distraction interrupted whatever the vampire was doing somehow, and Elijah simply died?

Who was she kidding, anyway, thinking she had a chance in hell of overpowering a being so old and powerful that he'd watched the pyramids being constructed? Elijah asked her to trust him—but she didn't trust *this*. She didn't trust *any* of this.

It's almost over, hayati, came the deep voice in her mind, layered with warmth and reassurance. She wanted to scream at him to keep his mind on what he was doing, damn it—but her breath was locked in her chest, her lungs burning as she held her breath, waiting for it to be done.

Finally, Elijah slumped in the strong arms holding him, his eyes rolling up until only a sliver of the whites showed. His face was gray; his lips tinged blue. Amy shuddered, pressing a hand to her mouth. Strong arms lifted him onto the medical cot where he'd so recently lain unconscious.

Her eyes were drawn to the molten bronze glow in Menkhef's eyes, and a moment later, to the red dripping from his fangs. One of them was slightly maloccluded, the professional part of her mind noted distantly, the vicious point displaying a few degrees of buccal torque.

He met her eyes over Elijah's unmoving body. *Not long now.*

Still the words were calm and reassuring. She wondered with a chill if he was influencing her somehow — making her stand here, silent and compliant, while he drank her husband's blood.

No, hayati. You feel only the aura that the others are spreading across the complex to try and hold the Darkness at bay. I will not overpower your will, just as I will not allow your humanity to be taken without your consent.

She thought of the Australian doctor, Mason, and of his baby nieces in Singapore.

"Not even at the cost of innocent lives?" she whispered.

He looked... so old, in that moment. Fresh tears spilled over Amy's cheeks.

Your humanity does not belong to me. It is not mine to barter for other lives, he said. *Perhaps if I were a kinder person, I would steal that choice from you and make it my own. But I cannot. Once I do so, the Darkness inside me wins.*

He looked down at Elijah, and Amy shivered as he tore into his own wrist, blood dripping from the jagged wound to splatter against Elijah's slack lips. For long moments, nothing seemed to happen... but then, Elijah's tongue darted out, tasting the red liquid. His eyes opened, and they were glowing. Amy caught her breath sharply as he grabbed Menkhef's arm and pulled it to his mouth, lapping and sucking at the gore, burying his teeth into flesh to widen the wound.

Amy didn't want to look... couldn't look away. It was primal, and ugly, and if it hadn't been for Menkhef's air of calm serenity as Elijah tore into his wrist with feral intensity, she was pretty sure she would have collapsed into screaming hysterics.

"All is well," he said aloud, though she wasn't sure which one of them he was speaking to.

Elijah continued to swallow the blood flowing from Menkhef's veins, until his movements grew slower and less coordinated, as though he were growing sleepy. Eventually, Menkhef eased his head down to the pillow and touched his forehead as though in benediction.

"Rest now, my guardsman," he murmured, and Elijah's eyes slid shut. With Elijah once more lying silent and still, he lifted his eyes to Amy's. "It is done."

Amy stared at Elijah's body for long moments. "He's not breathing," she whispered hoarsely.

"He no longer needs to," Menkhef said, sounding infinitely weary. "Come. Sit with him. But you must heed me when I warn you to back away. He will not be able to control his hunger when he first awakes."

That sounded… ominous. But she cautiously approached the cot and sat in the chair they'd pulled up to it for her earlier, when he'd been injured. Amy took his hand in hers. It was cool to the touch, and his complete stillness was more than a little disconcerting. But she'd seen him wake up and drink blood, just like they'd said he would. Menkhef had assured her that he was all right—that the transformation was successful.

Elijah was a vampire now.

"Did it work?" she asked. "Did making a twelfth vampire change anything?"

Menkhef's eyes went distant in the way she'd come to understand meant he was exercising his mental powers—seeing and hearing things she couldn't.

"There is no change," he said eventually. "The undead are still massing around the walls."

She was disappointed, but not surprised. "What are they waiting for? Why don't they attack while it's dark?"

Menkhef lifted a shoulder in an elegant half-shrug. "The enclave is protected by vampires. It will be far more strategically advantageous for them to attack after the sun is up."

"So we have a few more hours." A few more hours for her to torture herself with an impossible choice—the safety of her baby, or the safety of everyone else. Menkhef had been right earlier. It would have been kinder for him to take the choice out of her hands. Right now, she wasn't sure if she loved him or hated him for refusing to do so.

He watched her with an expression that said he knew exactly what she was thinking, and she had to look away, her eyes returning to Elijah's slack features. "You're certain he'll be okay?" she asked, aware of what a ridiculous question that was under the circumstances.

"He is arguably safer now than he was before," he replied.

She swallowed, trying to hold any further tears at bay. God knew they hadn't done her any good up to this point. "I suppose that's something, then," she said.

-o-o-o-

Several times over the course of the night, Menkhef urged her to leave the bedside and stand across the room by the door. Moments later, Elijah would awake and try to lunge for Amy's throat before she even had time to draw breath. She'd screamed the first time, but even before the shrill sound exited her lungs, Menkhef had already blocked Elijah with a hand splayed over his chest, pressing him back onto the bed as invisible energy crackled between them, raising the hairs on Amy's nape.

Mason had come in earlier that night with a cooler full of what Amy later learned were blood bags full of donations from humans like Shay, who had volunteered to feed the vampires. Each time Elijah regained consciousness, animalistic in his hunger, Menkhef fed him blood from the bags until he subsided into sleep again.

Above them, dawn was approaching. Amy had tried to distract herself as the hours passed by intermittently peppering Menkhef with questions about the past. He'd answered her every time, not shying away from her inquiries, but she got a sense that he was distancing himself from his answers. He replied with facts, but not emotions. Memories, but not the feelings associated with them.

"What happened to Nebetta's children?" she asked, remembering that with Heqab's help, she had eventually borne a boy and a girl.

"I do not know," he said, his eyes not lifting from Elijah's face, peaceful in sleep.

"They didn't die when Bael came for you, though?" she pressed.

"I did not kill them in my bloodlust," he told her, and she wondered how much his continued detachment was costing him.

"That's good, right?" she said. "They escaped, and went on to live their lives."

"Perhaps. Or perhaps the pharaoh hunted them down. If he found them, he would have had them executed or sold into slavery to ensure that my line could not continue, and that my lands would once again be under his control."

Her heart sank.

"No," came a faint rasp from the bed. Elijah's eyes opened, but they weren't glowing with un-thinking bloodlust this time. "I'd arranged for the servant, Sef, to hide them if anything ever hap-pened to all three of us. He took them upriver to another village, where they were to be raised as commoners by a family I knew. Sef was loyal—the pharaoh would never have been able to find them." He frowned. "I mean... Heqab did those things. Weird. Everything's running together in my head."

"Elijah?" Amy asked tentatively, hope swelling in her heart now that he seemed to have come back to himself.

"Amy?" He blinked up at her. "What happened? Are you all right?"

"I am now," she said, and watched as everything seemed to come back to him at once.

His nostrils flared. "I'm... really thirsty. I feel like I'm burning up."

Menkhef had grown silent and still when Elijah spoke about the past... about the children. But he roused himself now, leaning forward. "Feed from me, but try to maintain control this time. My blood will give you more strength than human blood, and I fear you may have need of that strength soon."

He offered his arm upturned, and Elijah's gaze caught on the blue-green roadmap of veins beneath the skin. His eyes kindled with a coppery glint, and fangs poked out from his gums as Amy watched in fascination. He took the offered wrist and dragged his gaze up to meet Menkhef's for a moment before he bit into it, drawing on the blood that welled up.

"I never knew what became of Iahmesu and Ehsret," Menkhef mused quietly as Elijah drank. "By the time Eris found me in my tomb, three thousand years had passed. If our children had survived to adulthood, any of their descendants would have been more than a hundred generations removed from me. Perhaps I could have searched and found some fragment of record about them. But I decided, in the end, that not knowing was preferable to finding that they had died young, or lingered in cruel servitude."

"It sounds like they had the same chance at life as any person has," Amy offered, picturing the two young children spirited away to a new life by a trusted servant. "Why not believe that they went on to be happy?"

Elijah forced himself to release Menkhef's wrist, and Amy watched as the twin wounds closed over in seconds. Menkhef cupped his cheek—a fleeting caress.

"Even in death, you watched over them," he mused. "I should not be surprised by this."

Elijah looked uncomfortable. "Not me. Heqab."

"His soul is yours," Menkhef said, the words stated as fact.

Reincarnation. Amy had never been all that religious, and she could barely wrap her brain around it even now. Could it be true that this whole situation—this whole war—hinged on the sort of love that drew lost souls to return over and over to the living world, searching for their missing pieces?

Suddenly, the underground room felt claustrophobic.

"Elijah, are you all right now?" she asked, bringing his knuckles to her lips and kissing them.

"I'm not sure *all right* is the word," he said. "But I feel like myself again, at least. My mind isn't burning any more."

She nodded. "I need to get out of these tunnels for a few minutes." She looked to Menkhef. "Is it safe?"

He smiled, but it was a sad expression. "No. It is precisely as dangerous as it would be if you remained here. Go, *hayati*. If you need help, call, and we will come."

Elijah tangled his fingers around hers, holding her in place as his eyes shot to Menkhef. "None of the other vampires will try to take matters into their own hands if she's alone?"

Christ. She was such a wreck right now, the thought hadn't even occurred to her.

Menkhef held his gaze evenly. "They will not. I have spoken with them, and we have an understanding in place. I trust each of them with my life. More importantly, I trust them with *your* lives."

She frowned. "You spoke with them? But you never left this room, and neither did I."

I do not need to leave this room to speak with them, nor they with me, he said inside her mind.

"Oh. Right. Still working on getting my head wrapped around that part—sorry." Amy thought of the way he'd barreled into the fight at the Headless Pyramid like a creature possessed, knocking undead creatures away from her like bowling pins and whisking her and Elijah away to safety. Even so, there was no real guarantee that one of his friends wouldn't take matters into their own hands. A tiny, unworthy part of her couldn't help thinking if they did, it would save her from having to make the impossible choice that faced her.

Elijah's brow furrowed, his expression unhappy, but not as worried as before. "I can see his memory of the conversation in my head. He... told them that turning you against your will would jeopardize the battle, and they believed him. They agreed not to."

"That's good enough for me." She kissed Elijah's hand again, though he looked troubled as she let his fingers slip free.

"Don't go far," he begged. "Come back the instant you sense trouble."

"I just need some air," she assured him. "I won't be long."

She could feel both of their gazes on her back as she left the room. She'd been more worried about Elijah than about paying attention to her surroundings when she'd arrived, but it wasn't too difficult to follow the line of hastily strung bulbs back to the landing, where steep stone steps led up toward the light.

At least, it *should* have been light outside. It was well past dawn by now, but the illumination was murky, and gusts of wind carried stinging dust through the compound. She climbed to the top of the imposing cobra head wall, wondering if there was a storm coming. Even in the Egyptian desert, there must be storms sometimes, she supposed. When she looked up at the sky, however, her breath caught as memories from another life bubbled up.

The sky roiled with thick, oily black fog. Not clouds, but something far worse. The memory of watching that smothering vapor descend into the courtyard of Menkhef's palace—burning her like acid as it swirled around her body—made her choke on a cry of dismay.

The demon was here, circling their desert refuge like a vulture circling prey.

TWENTY-ONE

Amy was so distracted by the horror floating above them in the sky that she didn't realize she wasn't alone on the windblown stone parapet at first. A woman she'd only noticed in passing when she'd stumbled in from the desert, desperate to get back to Elijah, stood at the end of the wall. Wild chestnut curls whipped around her face in the breeze, her loose white clothing billowing as she looked out across the compound spread out below them.

Amy moved to join her, suddenly wanting to be close to another person in the face of the Darkness looming over them, despite her earlier desire for a few moments of solitude. She looked down at the tents and other detritus of human occupation. From this height, it all looked hopelessly delicate — like a child's toys that might be knocked over and smashed at any moment.

The people who had come here to escape the wrongness creeping over the world were gathered in the open space, facing a low stone plinth. Three people sat cross-legged on the raised stone — a woman with two men flanking her. Amy looked closer, and thought she recognized Shay and the two guys she'd been talking and laughing with the afternoon when she and Elijah had first arrived. The three appeared to be leading the crowd in a chant, or maybe a prayer. Xander and Manisha stood watchfully at the back of the group, eyes scanning their surroundings for approaching danger.

The woman on the parapet next to Amy spoke without turning to look at her, eyes fixed on the seething sky above them. "Five hundred years ago," she said, "that creature tried to destroy the man I loved right in front of me. I didn't let it happen then, and I'm not going to let it happen now."

A lump formed in Amy's throat.

Another figure joined them on top of the wall—a striking man with black hair and silver eyes. Those startling eyes swept over Amy, sadness and resolve behind them. He stepped forward and wrapped the woman in his arms from behind. "Together, *draga mea*. We will face the battle together. All of us—stand or fall," he said in a calm, resolute voice. "Now, come away, please. It is not safe for you in the open with the sun already up. This kind of Darkness is no refuge for us."

"Just a minute more..." the woman said, and turned her head to meet Amy's eyes. "Is your husband okay now, Dr. Carpenter?"

Amy nodded uncertainly. "I... think so. He woke up a few minutes ago and seemed more like himself."

"That's fast," the beautiful vampire said. "He must be a strong person to have recovered so quickly."

"Stronger than me," Amy whispered, mortified to realize that fresh tears were welling up in her eyes.

Compassion flitted across the woman's lovely features, and she slipped free of her partner's arms to close the distance between them. To Amy's surprise, the vampire drew her into a tight embrace and rubbed her back soothingly.

"I somehow doubt that," she said.

"Why?" Amy managed.

"Because you're Snag's mate. Menkhef's, I mean. And I can't imagine him going for some kind of fading flower—now, or four millennia ago."

Amy squeezed her eyes shut, tears slipping free as she did. She realized, then, how close the vampire's teeth were to her neck, and again the irrational desire for the woman to *just fucking do it* and make it someone else's responsibility flashed through her thoughts.

"I'm scared," she admitted, as though that fact should come as a surprise to anyone at this point. "I am scared out of my goddamned mind right now, and it's all on me. *All* of it. I want so fucking badly to make the wrong choice, but I *know* it's the wrong choice." She looked up at the sky, not pulling away from the other woman's embrace. "I know what that creature is. I *remember*. I don't want to risk my child by letting Menkhef turn me. Though if I don't, I'll probably die during the battle, and then my baby will die with me. But... if we did somehow escape... if we survived, how could I even think about bringing an innocent life into a world ruled by that sadistic, horrible *thing*?"

She was weeping again, barely able to get the words out around her sobs.

The female vampire didn't try to shush her... didn't try to tell her what to do or offer meaningless platitudes. She just held her. The silver-eyed man approached them quietly and put a gentle hand on Amy's shoulder. Amy looked up at him, her vision blurred with tears.

"I don't have an answer for you," he said. "But I've known Menkhef for almost six hundred years... or rather, I *thought* I knew him. I have seen him protect those he cares about. I have seen him sacrifice for the innocent. But in all that time, I have never before seen him burn with such love for someone. Much less, *two* someones. Whatever choice you make, he will exert the last ounce of his power to protect you—and to protect the life you carry inside."

She already knew the right answer. She'd known the answer ever since the moment she truly accepted that Bael was coming to destroy the world. "I have to go," she rasped. "Let me go, please."

The woman's arms loosened, and the man's hand fell away.

"We'll come with you," said the female vampire. "We may not be able to do much, but we will damned well make sure that *nobody* faces this battle alone."

Amy nodded, the tiniest thread of comfort weaving through her panic upon hearing those words. She let the pair lead her back into the catacombs of the South Tomb, where they brought her unerringly to the room where Elijah and Menkhef were waiting. Elijah lurched to his feet when he saw the two vampires with her, his eyes flaring the color of molten metal.

"It's all right," she told him, knowing that she probably looked anything *but* all right, with her red, puffy eyes and cheeks wet from crying. "Elijah... I'm so sorry. But I can't condemn our child to a world where Darkness has overcome the Light. I just... can't do it."

"Amy! Are they controlling your mind?" Elijah demanded, still glaring daggers at the pair standing behind her. "*What did they say to you?*"

"They said that Menkhef would try to protect us no matter what choice I made." She swallowed hard. "And I choose to join the Council and fight." Her eyes slid to Menkhef, pleading. "Please, just... try to save my baby."

Menkhef rose to stand next to Elijah.

I will. The words echoed in her head.

"Amy, *no*," Elijah whispered.

She bit the inside of her cheek until her traitorous emotions calmed enough that she could speak without her voice trembling—but the words were still some of the most difficult she'd ever uttered. "I'm sorry, Elijah. I love you, but just as Menkhef couldn't make this decision for me... neither can you. I understand what's at stake, and I choose the risk."

Menkhef met the silver-eyed man's gaze over her shoulder. "Time is short. I need you, Eris, and Duchess." His expression went distant for a moment, presumably as he contacted the others. Then his deep eyes settled on Amy. "Come here, *hayati*."

She unlocked her knees by force of will and walked on shaky legs to the cot Elijah had vacated, settling on its edge. Elijah sat next to her and wrapped an arm around her shoulders.

"Do you forgive me?" she asked tremulously, looking up at her husband's face.

A harsh rush of air escaped his lungs. "Amy. I love you. There's nothing you could do that would make me stop loving you."

It wasn't exactly an answer, but she couldn't bring herself to press the issue. Menkhef gathered her hands between his. Though his skin was cool, she felt the hum of power along her nerves like tiny flames.

You must understand what you ask of me, hayati. I will have the strongest among us try to cushion the life inside you from danger with their power. But to ensure that I harm your body as little as possible, I must drain you slowly. In doing so, I will extend the agony of your soul being rent in two.

She'd relived Menkhef's turning at Bael's hands; felt what it meant to have one's soul torn into pieces. She'd watched Elijah writhing in pain, his mouth open around a cry too large to escape his lungs.

"I understand," she said. It didn't matter. All of her fear was tied up on behalf of others right now. She couldn't spare any for herself, but... "Will it hurt my baby the same way?"

One of Menkhef's hands untangled from hers to rest over her womb, still and grounding. "No. I will not touch your child's soul, my heart. Only yours."

A faint fluttering hitch vibrated against her side where Elijah was pressed against her—the feeling of someone ruthlessly forcing back tears. She leaned into him, squeezing closer against the curve of his body, and his arm tightened around her.

Other vampires arrived—an olive-skinned man Amy hadn't seen before, along with the Australian doctor, Duchess, and the black woman who'd helped rescue them from the zombies and then turned into an owl. Oksana, Chan had called her. Duchess looked as pale as a ghost, and she balked in the doorway. Her eyes slid over Amy and away, as though she couldn't bring herself to make eye contact.

"I can't do this, *grand frère*," she said. "I'm sorry. I know you've asked almost nothing of me over the centuries, but this task is beyond me. Forgive me."

"I'll act in her stead," Oksana said. "I'm not as old or as powerful, but when Mason was dying, I was able to wrap my life force around his and keep it from flickering out until help came. I know what to do."

Menkhef nodded. "I understand. I am sorry to have asked this of you, my sister. Oksana, your help is most welcome."

Duchess managed a tight nod in return before more or less fleeing the room. The man with dark Mediterranean features—who by process of elimination must be Eris—looked grim.

"We have an additional problem," he said. "I can sense Bastian Kovac's presence nearby."

"I am aware," Menkhef said, his features going stony with anger for an instant so brief, Amy wasn't totally sure she'd seen it.

"One crisis at a time," said the silver-eyed man. "Xander and Manisha are keeping watch above. They'll let us know as soon as anything happens."

"Who's Bastian Kovac?" Amy asked, more for distraction than anything else.

"The man behind the bombing in Damascus, among several other unsavory things," Eris said. "I suppose it was inevitable he'd be tied up in the endgame somehow."

Amy shuddered, thinking of the awful news reports about the terrorists' suitcase nuke. Elijah's arm tightened around her protectively.

"Are you ready, *hayati*?" Menkhef asked, his expression back in its smooth, unruffled lines.

"What the hell kind of question is that?" she asked, an odd feeling of detachment beginning to creep over her. "No, I'm not. Now, can we please do this before the world ends?"

He nodded, and his eyes flickered to Elijah's. "She will need my blood for strength, but she will need yours as well, for the love behind it."

Elijah glared at him. "I'd give the last drop of my blood to keep her safe," he grated out.

"I know," Menkhef said. "I promise you — while we live, she will never lack for blood."

Despite her fear, a lump rose in Amy's throat. She choked it down and let them position her lying back in Elijah's arms, cradled between his thighs with her head resting against the crook of his shoulder. Menkhef stood next to the cot on her right side, and the three vampires he had asked to help him protect her baby stood shoulder to shoulder on her left.

Oksana placed her hand over Amy's womb. Eris and the silver-eyed vampire covered it with theirs. All three closed their eyes. Amy couldn't feel anything where they touched her, but the hairs on her arms stood up, her skin prickling into gooseflesh.

"I love you," Elijah said, the choked whisper sounding broken against the shell of her ear.

"I love you, too. It—" She had to stop and swallow to steady her voice. "It'll be okay, Elijah. It has to be."

Menkhef lifted her right arm as though it was made of the finest glass. She refused to squeeze her eyes shut like a frightened child at the dentist's office, instead watching his face as he cradled her forearm. His eyes glowed with that strange inner light, and the points of fangs erupted as his lips drew back.

Her odd detachment had apparently returned, because she once again noticed the slight malocclusion of the left one.

"Did you know I'm an orthodontist?" she asked in a faraway voice. "I could totally fix that fang for you if… well… if we manage to live long enough to get back to civilization. And, you know, if the world doesn't end in a fiery apocalypse first." She trailed off, vaguely aware that she was babbling to distract herself from what was happening.

He paused, a look of painful fondness crossing his regal features. *I will keep it in mind*, he replied silently, pressing a kiss to the sensitive skin stretched over her veins. He cast a final, meaningful look at the three vampires huddled on her other side… and struck.

Amy gasped, bracing, but the pain of the wound was hidden under a sense of burning warmth that seemed to radiate outward from Menkhef's bite. The intense sensation hovered on the cusp between pleasure and discomfort. She was shocked and a bit mortified to find fire igniting in her belly. She squirmed in Elijah's arms, trying not to feel such a thing while three near-complete strangers were pressing their hands over her lower abdomen.

A moan slipped free from her lips, though she hoped it could credibly be ascribed to pain rather than… anything else. Elijah's arms tightened, and he let out a harsh breath that puffed against her temple. The burning sensation crept up her arm to her shoulder, and eventually flooded into her chest. Any question of it not being painful fled, and her heart stuttered before picking up the pace in a fluttering frenzy.

Lightheadedness swept over her, the room narrowing to a tunnel before turning gray around the edges, then red. She started to buck and struggle in earnest, but the hands holding her arm steady might as well have been iron bands. Elijah made a harsh sound and buried his face against her hair, but his arms around her didn't loosen.

"Careful, Snag," an Australian voice cautioned, though the words sounded like they was coming from underwater. "Take it slow now."

Agony erupted behind Amy's heart and lungs, unlike anything she'd ever experienced. She thought she screamed, but her hearing seemed to have gone away at the same time her vision closed in, until only impenetrable blackness remained. She panicked, certain that the demon had come for them… that it was too late. They would fall before its power, helpless as it pierced them with filthy claws and ripped out their humanity, leaving them as soulless puppets like the ones that had attacked her and Elijah.

Her throat hurt with the force of screams she couldn't hear, but then the sense of something vital being torn from her eased. Time slowed to a crawl, the fiery pain not receding, but not growing any worse, either. She tried to focus on the reasons she had to hang on, but her mind had been reduced to animal instinct. She would have bartered anything to make it stop—torn off a limb, thrown her loved ones to the wolves, all of it without a second thought.

An all-encompassing need was growing inside her. It was a thousand times worse than the most terrible drug addiction she could imagine. It wasn't just that if she didn't get what she needed, she would die. If she didn't get what she needed, the fucking *world* would burn.

Madness threatened—rose up to swallow her—and just as it was poised to devour her whole, the sweetest ambrosia that had ever existed dribbled between her lips. She roared, all her senses exploding back to life as she lunged for the source of the rich nectar. Arms fell away under the force of her struggles, and an instant later her teeth were latched onto cool flesh, ripping and tearing, desperate to make more of that nourishing liquid appear.

"*Amy!*" The choked cry came from behind her, but she ignored it.

She prepared to fight any attempts to pry her loose from her prize, but none came. A strong hand cradled her head in place, holding her lips to that source of salvation.

It's all right, hayati. Feed now, and deeply.

The mental voice was a cool wash of comfort, but it didn't touch the raging need inside her. Only the liquid pouring into her mouth and down her chin could do that. As the desperate craving began to ebb, she became aware of a second figure pressed against her back, sandwiching her between two tall forms. A rumble shook free from her throat, and she arched like a cat between them, rubbing her body with abandon as though she could mark both of them for her personal use.

When the flow of ruby blood from her first prize slowed to a trickle, she twisted, sliding sharp fangs into flesh the color of fine chocolate rather than dusky gold. Her new conquest groaned, a hard length sliding against her belly as his hips flexed.

"Fucking... *Christ*," he said, and she felt the strangled curse vibrate against her lips.

Drowsy lassitude slid over her as her sated stomach stopped screeching like an angry beast. She sagged, still held between the two strong men as her fangs slipped free from raw flesh.

"How is the child?" a hoarse voice asked from behind her, sounding exhausted beyond measure.

She knew something about the question was terribly, *life-changingly* important, and she tried to focus on the answer. It was no use, though, as weakness pulled her consciousness into the depths of a dark, endless ocean.

-o-o-o-

Amy was still floating when a different voice penetrated the cocoon of cotton wool surrounding her thoughts. This one was female, melodic, like a thousand bells chiming in harmony.

Wake, my child, it said, and Amy felt a sensation like a mother's hand stroking through her tangled and sweat-soaked hair. *You are needed. I will lend you strength to keep the blood-hunger at bay for now.*

Power not her own flooded through her body, bringing vitality to rubbery muscles and clarity to her decimated thoughts. Amy lunged upright, the stone room where she'd been turned into a vampire swimming into focus as memories slotted into place like puzzle pieces. A hand closed on her shoulder, the weight of command behind it keeping her from leaping off the blood-spattered cot she'd been lying on.

It wasn't blood she was after, though. "My baby?" she asked, her hands flying to her belly.

She was peripherally aware of the vampires around her exchanging looks of surprise, but then Elijah was there, cupping her face, pressing his lips to her forehead.

"Still alive," he whispered, and the world started turning again.

The Australian doctor approached cautiously, as though braced for her to go for his throat at any moment. "We can still sense the fetal life force, and with the benefit of vampire hearing, I was able to confirm with a stethoscope that the heartbeat is elevated but stable. That's not a guarantee that your body will be able to carry to term as a vampire, and it's definitely not a guarantee that any of us will be alive tomorrow to find out one way or the other. But for now, your baby is alive."

She sagged with relief.

"That being said," the doctor continued, "you're supposed to be out cold for hours, and mindless with hunger for at least the better part of a day." His slate blue eyes sought Menkhef, who was standing by the side of the cot. "Any thoughts on why that's not the case?"

Amy swallowed against the dryness of her throat. "There was a voice in my head. Female. She said I was needed and she'd lend me strength."

Before any of the others could respond, Duchess appeared in a hurry, slapping a palm against the doorframe to halt her momentum. Her expression was tense. "Xander says come quickly. Something's happening."

The general rush for the door was halted an instant later, when the same voice that had spoken to her before echoed through the stone chambers of the South Tomb, clear and beautiful.

I have come to you, my children. I hear your call, and I am here. But the final confrontation is almost upon us. If you are to prevail, you must first step into the Light.

TWENTY-TWO

Menkhef steeled himself to face this final battle in the face of his growing exhaustion, unwilling to seek nourishment from either his fellow vampires or the humans above when doing so might weaken them at a critical moment. He reached out to Israfael, trying to communicate, but gods and goddesses had never shown much interest in the thoughts of their game pieces. There was no response.

At least She had seen fit to spare Amy the aftermath of her turning. His two long-lost mates clung together for strength, just as it should be. If nothing else, Menkhef would carry with him the memory of holding Amy between his body and Elijah's after the worst of her torment had eased, but before her fangs had slid free from his throat. That sweet, fleeting moment would serve as his talisman through whatever came next.

He had his suspicions as to what that might be. If he was wrong, it seemed very likely that they would fall to Bael's creatures—becoming meat for the undead. And if he was right, they might well fall prey to their own natures, instead.

He needed to stay strong for just a bit longer.

"Come," he said, shaping his voice into something calm and commanding despite the burn of fatigue pulling at his bones.

Their group met Xander and Manisha at the entrance to the tunnels. They were ushering dozens of humans into the dubious protection of the tomb—many of them carrying small children or helping the elderly and infirm.

"That's it," Xander was saying, his voice determinedly calm. "Pardon the dust and gloom. Make yourself at home—several of the rooms have chairs and mattresses. And don't worry; this place has been here for more than forty-seven hundred years. It won't be going anywhere today."

Menkhef transformed into mist and swirled past the crush of humanity, aware of Tré and Eris doing the same behind him. They materialized next to Xander and Manisha. The young woman motioned them to one side of the tunnel with a jerk of her chin while her mate continued to reassure the people hurrying past.

"Something's happening in the sky," she said. "It started about five minutes ago. Beams of light are randomly breaking through the dark fog. It's not sunlight. The rays are coming from every direction and they're blinding, both to us and to the humans. As soon as we saw them, we brought everyone who wanted to come down here. The rest are sheltering in their tents, though the wind has picked up considerably in the last few minutes so I don't know how safe they'll be there."

"You did well," Tré said.

Xander joined them once the last of the humans had disappeared into the catacombs, and the other vampires came as well, once the way was clear.

"So," Eris said, eyeing the shifting patterns of light and shadow beyond the tunnel entrance with misgivings, "do we think stepping into the Light was meant as a literal directive, then?"

"Ah. You all heard the voice, too?" Xander asked, a wry twist entering his voice. "That's a relief. I thought maybe I'd finally cracked."

"We heard it," Eris confirmed, putting an arm around Trynn when she came to stand at his side. "The question becomes what we plan to do about it."

Xander took a deep breath and exchanged a look with Manisha. "It seems relatively straightforward from where I'm standing," he said. "As one of the least combustible people here, I'll volunteer to go out and check the UV rating."

"You mean *we'll* volunteer," Manisha said in a tone that brooked no opposition. "Your Victorian chauvinism is showing, my love."

Tré shook his head. "That will not be necessary, *tovarăş*," he began. "I should be the one—"

Menkhef did not allow him to finish. "I will go. Shield yourselves, and help the youngest protect their minds from whatever befalls me. If I survive, reopen the link and follow me one at a time."

"No, *wait*—" The voice was Amy's, and Menkhef met Elijah's eyes for the briefest of moments. As though they were in complete accord, Elijah nodded and took Amy's shoulders, gently restraining her from trying to come after him. Her eyes were full of such fear for him that it brought an ache to Menkhef's chest, but she subsided in her husband's grip, biting her lower lip in distress.

He let his gaze slide over the others, pausing last on Eris and Trynn.

"My old friend," Eris asked, "are you certain about this?"

"In the end, it seems I am certain of very few things," he replied truthfully, and strode out of the tunnels, mounting the stairs that led upward toward the light.

His instincts cringed from the crazy patchwork of blinding brilliance in the sky above, cutting swathes through the oily black mass of Bael's power. A quick mental scan of the surroundings beyond the walls showed undead numbering more than a thousand massed beyond the entrance, led by the only being in recent memory who had succeeded in rousing Menkhef to feelings of murderous hatred.

The black stain of Bastian Kovac's crippled soul stood ready to march his Dark troops into this fragile enclave, bringing horror to those who'd come seeking shelter and refuge. Still, Menkhef could make no move against his old enemy until Israfael's will had been done.

He stepped into the dazzling light, and burned.

Yet his body was not destroyed by Israfael's light. Rather than coming from his flesh, the agony came from within—from the darkest parts of his soul being illuminated for all to see. Every moment of hatred or despair. Every decision that caused innocents pain. Every werewolf who'd ever suffered because Menkhef had drunk from an innocent animal to sate his thirst. His failure to protect Sangye Rinchen, an innocent victim of Menkhef's own hubris. Every instance where his tendency toward secrecy and silence had placed his friends in danger.

His mental walls crumbled in the first instant, and he fell to his knees at the top of the cobra head wall, clutching one hand to his chest. He could sense the others experiencing his worst transgressions right along with him.

We can't shield against this, my friend, came Eris' warning. *We'll stand with you, though. Your darkness is ours, and all your sins toward us — if sins they truly were — are forgiven.*

Menkhef had never sought absolution in all these long and hopeless years. To do so had always felt as though it would somehow minimize the scope and breadth of his wrongdoings, both in his human life and after his turning. For this final battle to hinge on his ability to do just that seemed a cruel irony.

And he was so tired.

You're a good man. You were a good man in Egypt and you're a good man now. The feminine mental voice was unpracticed — both unfamiliar to him, and somehow better known to him than his own reflection.

His precious heart, lost for so long, and now found again.

There's a reason Heqab and Nebetta loved you more than they loved their own lives. A different voice. Male. And just as familiarly unfamiliar.

His noble soul—his guardsman—still watching over that which he held dear, so many millennia later.

Menkhef curled forward until his forehead rested on the cool sandstone of the parapet, letting the Light burn through him and illuminate every crevice... every dark nook and cranny left festering in the hidden corners of his injured spirit. And when it was done, the terrible scorching exposure of it eased, leaving him shaky. Lighter. Parts of him burned away to nothing.

We're still here. Eris' voice, filling his mind like a warm breeze.

Not going anywhere. Trynn, that time—stubborn and steadfast as ever.

Are you all right? Amy's unpracticed voice, thready with fear.

And... he was.

The Light had not destroyed him. His friends were still here.

Join me, he told them, rising on unsteady feet.

Eris strode up from the tomb—his oldest friend, and his savior twice over. The younger vampire cried out in pain as the Light shone into him. Menkhef steadied him, lending him strength as Israfael exposed every selfish and greedy impulse of the former tomb robber. Every grave he'd ever desecrated in the pursuit of art and money. Every display of impatience and short temper. Every unworthy impulse. Every drop of blood stolen from an unsuspecting mortal.

When it was over, Eris leaned heavily on him for a moment, head hanging and face pale. The others followed, joining them one by one.

Trynn, with her arrogance and her burning, bone-deep hatred for Bastian Kovac, the man who had tortured her mate nearly to the point of death.

Tré's scorching—and largely irrational—sense of failure in his self-imposed duties of leadership. His certainty that left up to him, the war against Bael would have been lost. His ruthlessness. His zeal in hunting humans for blood during the early decades after his turning.

Della's unspoken guilt over having allowed her parents to believe she'd died during the violence in New Orleans.

Oksana's deeply rooted self-loathing for the monster Bael made her—a loathing that had led her to punish her body by forcing food and drink into it over the centuries, despite the unbreakable curse that only allowed her to consume blood without pain.

Mason's sense of having abandoned the children in Haiti he'd sworn to care for. His sickening fear over having placed his brother's family in danger by convincing them to open an enclave in Singapore—an enclave now surrounded by an undead army poised to strike them down.

Xander's continued guilt over the suffering he'd allowed in his London factories during the Industrial Revolution—children exploited to line his own pockets with money.

Manisha's feelings of worthlessness after being unable to save a young boy she'd considered to be under her care. Her fervent wish that she could have been the one to die in Sangye's place.

Elijah came forward reluctantly. Menkhef could feel his uncertainty about the reception he was likely to receive from this tight-knit group... this unlikely family of choice. He gasped as the burning Light illuminated his desire to give up—on *everything*.

On his career. His marriage. And, in the depths of night when his terrible despondency of the spirit was at its worst... his desire to give up on his own life. To end things permanently.

The revelation threatened to shatter Menkhef's frail and battered heart. He and Eris caught Elijah as his body sagged. Eris eased back after a moment, and Menkhef turned the support into an embrace, feeling Amy's love for her husband crash through both their minds like a runaway chariot team.

No more despair, Menkhef silently assured the shaking man. *We'll make a new world, my guardsman—right here, right now. A new start for both of you.*

Wetness trickled into the dip of his collarbone, and he knew that should he look down, he would find rust-colored tears pooling there.

Amy rushed toward them, and they both caught her when Israfael's power shone on her horror at herself for having willingly risked her unborn baby's life... her belief that her impossible decision made her unfit to ever be a mother or a wife to anyone.

"No," Elijah rasped, pressing her between them as he'd done after Menkhef turned her. "It makes you the bravest and most selfless person I've ever met. I love you so much it hurts."

"I thought you'd never forgive me," she sobbed. "I thought you'd never even want to look at me again."

"No, Ames… no, no," Elijah crooned, murmuring against her hair as they both wept openly.

Menkhef closed his eyes against all the pain that this long war—this endless chess game between gods—had wrought in the world. The other vampires were also embracing each other; grasping hands and wiping away each other's tears. Only Chan and Duchess remained behind.

Go, he heard Duchess tell her mate, a terrible desolation behind the word.

Chan hesitated before mounting the steps reluctantly, like a man walking to the gallows. Oksana and Mason broke apart from the others to meet him, and supported him when the Light tried to drive him to the ground. He shuddered as his darkest secret was dragged into the open— infidelity, continuing even after his human wife had fallen pregnant. She had discovered it, and left him. He'd barely had a chance to know his own daughter.

She remarried, mon coeur, came Duchess' mental voice. *And if he was your friend, it must mean he's a good man. You told me he loved your daughter like she was his own. He raised her as a father should—he even adopted her. Your infidelity freed Janette from an unhappy marriage to you, and allowed her to find happiness with another.*

Chan collapsed to his knees, covering his face with one hand as Mason and Oksana followed him down. They sat with him quietly as he gasped like a man surfacing from drowning, Duchess' words finally forcing him to see his actions from a different perspective.

Duchess stood alone now at the mouth of the tunnels, that bottomless sense of desolation from earlier leaking through gaps in the mental shield she was trying to hold around her innermost self. Menkhef frowned as she started up the stairs, step by slow step, as though being dragged forward by a rope tied around her waist. He let his arms fall away from Amy and Elijah, whose emotions were finally calming as they continued to hold each other.

Menkhef's eyes met first Oksana's, and then Xander's. Both looked as worried as he felt. They rose and headed to meet Duchess, Oksana leaving Mason behind to support Chan as he recovered.

My sister, Menkhef sent, trying to reach her through the heavy barrier she was struggling to maintain, *you must let your walls crumble. You are not strong enough to resist the goddess' pull; you will only cause yourself more pain by resisting Her.*

The Light reached Duchess at the same moment Xander and Oksana did. She gasped, her face set in hard lines, wisps of steam sizzling from her skin as she fought not to let the beam penetrate into her soul, leaving it to ravage her flesh instead.

"*Ti mwen!*" Oksana cried, as she and Xander tried to shelter her with their bodies. "Don't fight it! You'll hurt yourself!"

"Duchess," Xander murmured, *"don't do this.* No matter what it is, it's not worth your life."

Chan was struggling to his feet, his own pain forgotten as he tried to get to his mate. Duchess cringed back, refusing to meet his gaze—only Oksana and Xander's grip keeping her from tumbling right back down the stairs she'd just ascended. Chan skidded to a halt, stark fear on his face.

"Marie—no." His voice was a bare croak. "I don't care what it is. Please, you have to believe me. Whatever it is… *I don't care.*"

Alarmed, Menkhef strode across to join them as the faint smell of burning flesh wafted across the parapet. He pushed close and took Duchess' face in his hands, his dark eyes boring into her distraught blue ones.

"Stop," he said softly, "we will not allow you to sacrifice yourself out of fear. *Let us in.*"

She squeezed her eyes shut to avoid his gaze, but her shields cracked nonetheless, pain spilling out through the gaps like blood. All at once, he could see her secret shame in the harsh Light of Israfael's power.

"My Darkness will break the Council," she whispered.

"It will not," Menkhef promised her. "Tell us now, and be free of it."

Her chest shook with sobs as she choked, "In the months before he sacrificed his life to save my soul from Bael… when Bertrand had gambled all our money away and first forced me into a life of treason, spying for the king's brother, I…" Her throat closed up until the words were almost inaudible. "I wished him dead. I thought... if he were killed on the king's business... I would get his pension, and I could marry again, or perhaps return to my father. My baby would not be born into poverty and constant fear, with a spy for a mother."

Menkhef wiped her tears away with his thumbs, and eased out of the way as Chan enveloped her in his arms, rocking her.

"I wished you dead, Wei Yong," she sobbed into his neck, "and then, I killed you."

"I told you," he said hoarsely. "I don't care. It's in the past, and I don't care about any of it, Marie."

Duchess clung to her mate with all of the desperation that she'd been holding inside for four centuries, and the Light no longer burned her skin. Menkhef felt the others' support swirl around her through their bond, and added his own to the mix.

When her shuddering tears subsided, the thirteen vampires gathered together, standing shoulder to shoulder as they looked out across the pyramid complex and the desert beyond. Above them, the Light grew stronger, more beams breaking through Bael's swirling Darkness as Israfael's chiming voice rolled over the courtyard.

Now you understand the nature of the final battle, my children. It was never a battle at all.

Menkhef felt confusion echo through the bond, and realized that the others still hadn't solved the puzzle. This was confirmed a moment later, when Xander raised a quizzical brow and said, "Er... that might be something of an optimistic conclusion, actually. The understanding part, I mean."

The ground rumbled, bits of stone shaking loose from the pyramid and rattling their way down to the bottom.

"Also the 'not a battle' part," Trynn muttered under her breath.

The atmosphere sparked with electric potential, and Menkhef narrowed his eyes as the makeshift barricade that Xander, Manisha, and the humans had tried to erect across the compound's only entrance exploded outward in a shower of wood and stone.

Bastian Kovac stood framed in the gap, power sizzling around him and Bael's undead army at his back.

Well, *bugger*," Xander observed. "Now things are going to get *really* interesting."

TWENTY-THREE

"Stand with me," Menkhef told the others, "But make no move toward violence. The fate of the world depends on it."

Then, knowing that the time for secrecy and silence was long past, he let his conclusions about Bael, the Angel, and the war they'd been waging flow freely through the bond. Shocked silence reigned for a long moment before Eris breathed, "*Oh*," and Xander murmured, "Right. Bloody hell—of *course* they are. Son of a *bitch*."

"We're with you," Tré assured Menkhef. "It's time to end this."

Menkhef lifted his chin and led the way down the steps from the top of the cobra head wall to the esplanade below. He walked toward Bastian Kovac with steady strides, allowing no hint of weakness to show in his bearing.

Bael's lieutenant radiated power. It crackled around him like a dark halo as he led his army into the complex. Menkhef continued forward to meet him, his comrades arrayed behind him. Sparks erupted between the two groups as their auras clashed. Kovac raised a hand, calling his undead forces to a halt, and Menkhef stopped as well, the other vampires in perfect synchrony with him.

Bael's creature—the being that had tortured Menkhef's oldest friend and destroyed an entire city with fire and poison—tilted his head, regarding him across the short span separating them.

"So," he said in his heavy, Eastern European accent, "you have found your thirteen bloodsuckers and formed your council. Yet you appear to have gained no new powers... acquired no new strength. I will take the utmost pleasure in making you watch as my Master's army rapes and consumes the fragile humans cowering in their tents and hiding in your underground tunnels like rats. Then, I will take just as much pleasure in personally finishing what I started with that one—" His eyes flicked to Eris. "—and repeating the process until each of you have watched your mates suffer, then perished yourselves."

Trynn made a sound like a snarl, but both Menkhef and Eris whipped mental power around her before she could lunge for Kovac. He could feel her trembling with rage, but she controlled herself, not making a move toward their old enemy.

Menkhef turned all of his attention back to the creature in front of him, and let a faint smile spread across his features.

"There will be no battle today, I fear," he said mildly.

Bastian frowned.

"Perhaps not, nightcrawler," he said, baring yellow teeth. "After all, from where I'm standing it looks more like a slaughter than a true battle."

Menkhef only raised an eyebrow. "Then you should focus less on what is in front of you, and more on what is above you. Israfael is not warring with Bael. She is merging with him. They are two parts of the same being — a universal force that was in balance until it was catastrophically split into two pieces, millennia ago."

Since that time, the dark part — Bael — had been leaving a trail of victims suffering the same agonizing wound he himself had suffered… the Darkness and Light inside them torn asunder. A broken creature lashing out, repeating the horrors of its past in unspoken — perhaps even unconscious — desperation to understand its own pain.

"Lies!" Kovac spat. "My Master would never join with a creature so sickeningly weak and saccharine! You seek only to delay the inevitability of your own demise."

Menkhef felt a wash of pity for the broken puppet before him.

"Indeed? Ask yourself why your *master* did not order you to lead your forces into our domain while we were weakened by Israfael's Light," he suggested, still in the same mild tone. "Ever since Bael realized the true meaning behind the prophecy, he has not sought our destruction directly. He has sought us as test subjects — beings suffering the same injury he suffers. Souls divided into Light and Dark."

Eris stepped up to Menkhef's side, undaunted as he faced his former tormenter. "Don't you *see*, Kovac? He couldn't use you, or any of his other undead puppets. Your soul is torn, but you don't seek to repair the damage. Instead, you revel in it. Only we vampires have sought some means of repairing the injury done to us — some way to make ourselves whole again. And with the return of our lost loved ones and our acceptance of our own Darkness, we have finally succeeded in healing."

Kovac's lips curled back in a snarl. "Fabricated drivel!" he spat. "Bael is perfect in his Darkness. He will destroy this cloying Light and rule the world! I will stand at his right hand, and finally receive everything I deserve!"

Trynn came to stand on Eris' other side, her narrowed eyes cutting through Kovac as though he were nothing. "Somehow," she said, "I very much doubt that."

Her gaze rose to the sky, and Kovac's followed it, as though he couldn't help himself. Above them, the Light and Dark were swirling together, merging and joining into a breathtaking dance of shadow and brilliance. The wind rose higher, whipping at them.

"No," Kovac said. "*I refuse to believe it.* My Master would not betray me in such a way..."

But the maelstrom of color and shadow was whirling even faster now, condensing and shrinking as the two forces canceled each other out.

"D'you think?" Trynn asked sweetly. "Because it kind of looks to me like he would."

Kovac growled and pulled an iron dagger from its sheath, the undead creatures at his back shifting in readiness to attack. Menkhef tilted his head, appraising the man who had roused him to vengeful bloodlust by harming those he cared about.

"Bastian Kovac, servant of Bael," he said, the words quiet but utterly sincere. "I forgive you."

At the same moment, the last of the dark clouds marking Bael's presence dissipated into nothingness, as the reunified force that had been split into two halves for so long disappeared from the mortal realm with a crack like thunder. Disbelief spread across Kovac's features as he realized that his idol had, in fact, abandoned him, followed by terror as he understood exactly what that meant for one whose only tie to the living world was the Darkness inside him.

A scream of rage tore free of Kovac's chest as his connection to his creator snapped. His flesh split and peeled, both he and the undead creatures under his command crumbling into dust before the vampires' eyes. The iron dagger clattered to the ground, abandoned. Wind gusted around the esplanade, blowing the powdery remains of Bael's army away to join with the desert sands.

There was a beat of absolute silence.

It was broken by Xander's sharply indrawn breath. "*Shit*... the sun! The rest of you need to get under cover *right now*—"

Indeed, the sky above them was now clear and blue. The sun was a fiery yellow orb above the eastern wall of the compound, visible to the right of the pyramid. But the light did not burn their flesh. Instead, Menkhef felt it like a warm caress on the side of his face. He closed his eyes, savoring the sensation of the rays against his skin.

Our gift in exchange for your faithful service, came a melodic, androgynous voice, sounding paradoxically both distant and achingly immediate. *You have stepped into the Light, and it can no longer harm you.*

"Oh. Good. That's good..." Menkhef murmured, as the crushing exhaustion he'd been holding at bay finally demanded its moment. A quick mental check ensured that Amy and Elijah were unhurt, standing a few steps away from him in the golden sunlight. Satisfied by that fact, Menkhef was only vaguely aware of his knees giving way. He was out cold before his body hit the ground.

TWENTY-FOUR

Six days after the world failed to end, Amy sat next to the familiar medical cot in the underground tomb at Saqqara, staring at strongly sculpted features that seemed ageless and ancient even in repose. She'd been doing a lot of that over the past several days—sitting here, watching Menkhef's motionless form, sometimes holding his hand and sometimes rising to pace restlessly around the stone chamber, her thoughts churning in endless circles.

He wasn't even breathing, damn it. And yeah, yeah, the others had reminded her repeatedly that as a vampire, he didn't need to breathe. But, well, it was the *principle* of the thing, all right? No one should be that... *still*.

Elijah wandered in, stretching, and came up behind her chair to place his hands on her shoulders and press a kiss to the top of her head. "Break time, Ames. I'll take over until sunset. Any change this morning?"

She shook her head. "I don't think so. Though... I was trying to concentrate earlier like Eris showed us, and I think maybe I felt him dreaming. It was hard to tell. I could have been imagining it, or maybe sensing someone else's thoughts instead of his."

Elijah sighed and dragged a second chair next to hers, dropping into it. He leaned forward, resting his elbows on his knees, and cocked his head at the figure on the bed. "You know, old man," he told the unconscious form, "when most people say they're so tired they could sleep for a week, they *don't mean it literally*. It's absolutely crazy out there. I expect the others could use your help with some of this shit."

"Any news worth passing on from the past few hours?" Amy asked.

Elijah brightened. "Yes, actually. We finally got a satellite link to Singapore. Mason's brother and his family are okay." He sobered. "They had about a dozen injuries and two deaths at the enclave—the wind blew down a large tent with some people inside, and there was a married couple who tried to make a run for it before the final battle. The pair of them ended up walking right into a group of zombies. But... given that there were almost a thousand people sheltering there, it could have been a lot worse."

"Yeah," she agreed. "It could have. Thank god Mason's nieces are all right—and his brother and sister-in-law, too." She shivered, unable to help herself. The married couple who'd died... it could have been her and Elijah. They'd come so close. Hanging onto survival by their fingertips—quite literally—before rescue had come in the form of the vampire lying on the cot before them.

The aftermath of the *battle-that-wasn't* had been a confusing tangle of relief that they'd somehow survived—that they'd somehow *won*—and terror when Menkhef had crumpled to the ground like a marionette with its strings cut. Eris and Trynn were closest; they'd been the ones to grab him and keep his skull from bashing into the dusty stone of the esplanade. Amy and Elijah had lunged forward the moment they saw his knees buckle. Amy thought she might have cried out some kind of denial at the feeling of Menkhef's mind folding in on itself and disappearing from her awareness like an old-fashioned TV monitor powering off.

She'd snarled at Eris and Trynn—a feral, animal noise that seemed to rise from nowhere. An instinctive, gut deep reaction to seeing someone cradling that broken form who *wasn't her or Elijah.* She was still more than a little mortified, thinking back on it, but neither Trynn nor her mate seemed to have held it against her. Eris had done something with his mental power that snapped her back to a more rational sort of awareness, keeping her from doing anything truly awful like trying to tear them away from Menkhef physically. Elijah skidded to his knees next to her an instant later, his hands closing around her shoulders convulsively.

"What happened, what's wrong with him?" he snapped, having evidently been more successful than she was at holding onto to little concepts like *language* and *asking reasonable questions.*

She was distantly aware of the other vampires gathering around them in a half circle, looking on with concern.

A horrible realization slid into Amy, and her hand flew to her mouth. "It was me, wasn't it?" she said, her voice coming out high and reedy. "I drained him. I drank too much of his blood and weakened him!"

Trynn actually snorted. "Yeah—no offence, kiddo—but get over yourself. I've seen him drained, and this isn't what it looks like. Eris, what the hell has he done to himself this time?"

Eris freed one hand and placed it on Menkhef's forehead, his expression growing distant as he concentrated. Amy held her breath, and noticed a moment later that Menkhef wasn't moving *at all*. As in, his chest wasn't rising or falling. He wasn't breathing.

"Is he—" she began, having to force the words past paralyzed lips.

"Sleeping," Eris interrupted mildly. "He's sleeping."

"Are you fucking kidding me?" Xander asked, as a general relaxation of tension swept through the group.

Mason squeezed past her to crouch near Menkhef's shoulders. "Just normal sleep? You're certain, Eris?"

Eris removed his hand and sat back on his haunches. "I'm not certain that *normal* is the applicable word, since to my knowledge, he hasn't slept in more than sixteen centuries. But, yes, he's merely resting in the arms of Morpheus. In the temporary way, I hasten to add—not the permanent one."

Around them, the humans who had been sheltering from the clash of otherworldly forces were creeping out of their tents and emerging from the tunnels, blinking in the bright morning light. Amy was reeling, her mind pulled in a dozen different directions. She and Elijah had been pulled into this close-knit cadre of individuals during the worst kind of crisis imaginable. She'd seen their innermost selves exposed, and they had seen hers. She'd learned that her husband had contemplated suicide and—god help her—she'd never even known about it.

She had no idea what state the world was in beyond the walls of the complex. Undead monsters had ravaged Saqqara village the previous night. Had the same thing happened around the world? Were her parents okay? Were Elijah's? Her friends? Her coworkers? Her clinic back in Pennsylvania? Would her baby survive to term, now that she was a vampire?

More than anything in the world, she wanted to collapse into hysterics in Elijah's arms. She swallowed hard, and craned to look over her shoulder at the silver-eyed vampire, Tré, who'd led his friends for centuries with courage and honor, all while thinking himself completely unworthy to do so.

"What do we do now?" she asked. "I want to help."

Tré met her gaze with perfect understanding… the sort of understanding that usually only came from being family, or through close friendship forged by the fires of shared danger.

"I need you and your husband to take shifts watching over Menkhef while he recovers," Tré said. "Mason and Oksana, check for injuries among the humans and treat them if necessary. Xander and Manisha, we need to find out what's happening elsewhere in the world. See if the satellite connection is still working, and find out what you can. Eris, Trynn, Duchess, and Chan—with the attack on Saqqara village, it's likely our supply chains for food and water are broken. We'll need to acquire both from whatever sources you can find nearby. See if the village is habitable. We may need to move these people there to simplify things. Della and I will coordinate from here and lend aid as needed once we have a better idea of what's happening outside the walls."

Everyone nodded, and Eris glanced between Amy and Elijah. "Need a hand getting him to a bed?"

Elijah eyed Menkhef's tall form for a moment. "I could probably manage him in a fireman's carry, but I doubt it would be very dignified for either of us," he said uncertainly.

"We'll get a stretcher," Mason said. "You're sure my skills aren't required, Eris?"

"He truly is just sleeping," Eris reassured. "Albeit quite deeply."

Mason shrugged. "After sixteen hundred years, I guess he must've needed it. Back in a tick."

Mason returned with the promised stretcher, and they moved Menkhef down to the catacombs again. Amy hurried ahead and pulled the bloody bedding off the cot where she'd been turned into a vampire mere hours ago. Once Menkhef was settled, Mason gave her and Elijah an assessing look and returned with a couple of bags of blood.

Even through the plastic, the smell was enough to overcome Amy's instinctive aversion to the idea of drinking human blood in the space of a heartbeat. Maybe the Angel hadn't been lying about sparing her the mindless bloodlust of her turning, but she still fell on the bag with ravenous hunger, aware that Elijah was doing much the same.

Self-consciousness didn't return until the bag was empty and she realized that she had torn it open so she could turn it inside out and lick up the last traces from the plastic. Mason had already left to check on everyone else, but Eris was still there with them. He took the torn bags, only asking, "More?" without a trace of judgment in his tone.

Amy tried to listen to her stomach before answering. The ache was gone, so she said, "No, thank you... I think I'm all right now. Elijah?"

"I'm good," Elijah confirmed. "No lingering urges to jump on anything with a heartbeat."

Eris nodded solemnly. "Then I'll leave you to watch over him. Can you still feel the link between us?"

Amy flushed, remembering all she'd seen and felt from the others along the strange mental bond. Gamely, she attempted to look inside herself, not entirely sure what she was looking for. Something in her mind vibrated like a plucked violin string.

"You felt that?" Eris asked. "That's the bond. Now try to reach me along it."

Hello? Amy thought tentatively, focusing intently on that odd inner connection.

Very good, Eris replied in the same way. *Elijah?*

Amy felt Elijah's attempt to speak through the bond much more clearly and immediately. *Yes, I hear you.*

"Well done," Eris said aloud. "It is likely that Tré and Della will be nearby, at least for the next several hours. But if you need something and can't easily find one of us, call along the bond and someone will come."

"Okay," Elijah said. "Good to know. Thanks."

Eris smiled, though there was a certain amount of tension behind it. They were all feeling it, Amy knew, and would be until they found out more about the state of things in the world at large. Eris reached a hand down to brush the tousled black strands of Menkhef's hair from his brow. This time, Amy saw it for what it was—a brother's love—and her protective instincts stayed quiet.

Eris seemed to pause as though debating whether to say anything more. When he did, his voice was quiet. "Look after him for me, please. I know that your circumstances are complicated, and only the three of you can decide how you wish to move forward. But... although he may not show it outwardly, he needs you both. *Badly.*"

Amy's eyes were drawn to Elijah's, where she saw the same uncertainty that was almost certainly reflected in her own. She drew breath to speak, only to pause, not knowing what to say to Eris' words. But when she dragged her eyes away from her husband's, Eris was already gone.

"There's time now, Ames," Elijah said softly. "It's all right. Somehow, we'll figure it out."

They'd stayed with Menkhef and talked. For *hours*.

They talked about Elijah's terrible admission—that he'd considered suicide and never told anyone... never sought help.

"Do you still feel that way?" Amy asked him, her voice quavering.

He took both her hands in his. "No, Ames. As soon as you got pregnant, I knew I could never go through with it. And now—even though it seems crazy with everything that's happened—I feel different, somehow. I feel... *hope*. I have no idea what's going to happen next, but somehow, for the first time in years... I want to find out."

She closed her eyes in relief, only to open them a moment later so she could stare into his. "Good. Because, Elijah? If you died, I'd just find you again when you were reborn and start over. Look around us. Look at what we've seen in the past couple of days. It turns out that for true love... *death is not the end*. And, realizing that? Well... I think it's just changed our lives forever."

He'd kissed her, with a passion she hadn't felt from him in years. If they'd been alone, she would have started tearing clothing off of him there and then. A deep-buried part of her whispered that she should do it anyway... that Menkhef wouldn't mind. But newly animalistic vampire instincts or no, going from a thoroughly vanilla marriage—and in recent months, a largely sexless one—to doing the nasty while locked in a room with an unconscious man was a step too far.

Okay, it was *several* steps too far.

But, *damn*. That kiss. When they pulled back in favor of resting their foreheads together, Elijah's hand tangled in her messy curls, they were both breathing hard.

"Vampires don't need to breathe, *my ass*," she whispered.

And then they were chuckling; snickering like two teenagers trying not to get caught while making out in the shadows, the laughter completely inappropriate for the circumstances, the surroundings, and the topic of conversation.

"I love you, Amy," Elijah said once they'd regained control. "I won't leave you, and I want you to be happy, even if *happy* doesn't end up looking like either of us expected it to look. I don't know what's going to happen now. I don't know if vampires can teach university classes or run dental clinics, or if those things will even exist in whatever the world has become now. But it's time for both of us to stop compromising with our lives. It's time for us to figure out what we want, and make it happen."

"I like that," she told him, still resting her head against his. "I like that a lot, Elijah. No more compromising. No more *scraping by*. It's time to live now."

Six days later, she still felt the same way, even though there were so many things hanging over them. Her body was still clinging to the pregnancy, but there were no guarantees. Neither of them had been able to contact their families yet. Menkhef still hadn't woken up. Daily life had become a near constant struggle to make sure that the humans in

Saqqara had safe food, water, and shelter until some sort of transportation and communications infrastructure was up and running again. And yet, like Elijah, she felt hope for the future.

Humanity was in a sort of collective worldwide shock in the days since skies across the globe had gone dark with swirling black fog, and the undead had marched on the living. Only a tiny fraction of the population had fled to the network of enclaves set up at spiritual sites around the world. The rest had done what people always do, pretending nothing was wrong until the crisis showed up on their doorstep.

And it had.

Saqqara had not been the only place where the undead had attacked en masse. The geographical pattern was sporadic, but from what they'd been able to determine through the spotty news reports and satellite phone contacts, any area near an enclave had become a hunting ground for the zombies to increase their numbers in preparation for the final confrontation.

Eris hypothesized that Bael thought the show of force threatening Israfael's most devoted supporters would help draw Her into the open. It was sobering to think that by offering a refuge for people seeking the Light, they had indirectly placed the humans around them in heightened danger. Amy had been struggling these past days to reconcile her hatred of a creature that had caused so much pain and death in the world with the understanding that Bael was damaged on a fundamental level.

Was being damaged somehow supposed to make it all okay? As the reported death toll rose and the full scope of what had been done to the world became clearer, it sure as hell didn't feel okay.

Outside of the enclaves, the undead hadn't been the only agents of chaos. When things started to go sideways, terrorists and other malcontents had come crawling out of the woodwork, adding to the violence and destruction. Riots had broken out in most major cities when the sky went dark, and something about the power raging in the sky had played havoc with power grids and communications systems. Even a week later, the only reliable methods for reaching far-flung areas were satellite and ham radio.

Amy decided that the only thing to do was to narrow her focus to what she could personally influence, and work on that. The alternative was to fret and agonize and waste energy on things that might or might not have happened. She was sick with worry over her friends and family in the United States, but she couldn't do a single thing to help them until phone and internet service was in better shape.

She could help with things in Saqqara, though. She could work on her relationship with Elijah. She could make sure Menkhef wasn't alone while he rested and healed from whatever had made him collapse. So that's what she did.

She and Elijah instituted a sort of informal shift system. For roughly a third of the day, he went out to lend whatever aid was needed at any given moment—hauling loads of food, scavenging fuel to run the generators that powered the water pumps in Saqqara village, manning the shortwave radio, maintaining the solar panels, and so forth and so on.

Then he would come back to Menkhef's chamber and spell her so she could sleep for a few hours on the mattress they'd jammed into the corner of the room. She would get up and do the same for him, and when they'd both gotten enough rest to be functional, she'd leave Elijah alone with Menkhef and venture out to do her own stint of volunteer work. So far, the most excitement had come when a middle-aged man who'd been staying at the complex got a tooth abscess, and she'd had to do an extraction with minimal access to medical supplies.

With Elijah safely back for the day and noon nearly upon them, tiredness washed over Amy like a gentle tide. She was finding it harder to stay awake during the height of the daylight hours now that she was a vampire, though the others assured her the effect would fade with time. She yawned widely, and Elijah shot her a crooked smile.

"Get some rest, Ames," he said.

A different sort of yearning hit her. "Will you sit with me for a while?" she asked, feeling a bit shy even though it was ridiculous to feel that way. "Hold me while I sleep?"

Elijah's eyes darkened, only to be lit up a moment later with glowing pinpricks of copper light. "Always," he said.

She leaned across and kissed him, feeling her eyes burn with their own inner light. It was almost as though they were courting again—reveling in the slow seduction of kisses and caresses, but holding back from more. She'd thought about bringing it up; making use of their seemingly newfound willingness to communicate like actual adults. But she hadn't.

Truth be told, she was enjoying it too much to want to analyze it to death, at least for the moment. It would be another thing entirely if their intimacy was still restricted to necking like teenagers a month from now, but this stage of their rekindling relationship felt to her like something that had a distinct end date. When Menkhef woke up, everything would change. How it would change, she still had no idea. But that was the event that would shake up the puzzle pieces inside their box. It was anybody's guess how those pieces would fit together afterward.

Amy let Elijah lead her to the mattress in the corner. It was a bit cramped with both of them on it, but she wasn't about to complain. She took the side nearest the wall, while he stuffed a battered pillow behind his shoulders and arranged himself in an easy sprawl, half-propped against the wall at the head of the makeshift bed.

With her cheek resting on his chest, her leg slung over his, and his hand stroking up and down her arm, she let herself exist completely in the moment, all of their other cares and concerns falling away. She knew those cares would still be there later, when she was ready to pick them up again.

"Jus' for a few minutes," she slurred, sleep already tugging at her.

"Sleep, Ames," Elijah said, his voice a low rumble against her cheek. "I can see the cot just fine from here if he starts to wake up, and I can't think of anywhere else I'd rather be right now than holding you."

Amy made a sleepy noise, and burrowed closer against him.

TWENTY-FIVE

In the dream, Amy was in Menkhef's palace in Ancient Egypt, but when she caught a glimpse of her bare arm, her skin was its usual pale expanse of freckles rather than Nebetta's rich, golden brown tones. She was pressed between two bodies, her head lolling to the side in wanton abandon as lips and teeth worried at the tender skin of her neck from behind.

"You have no idea what you do to me, *hayati*," murmured the deep voice that had worked its way into the depths of Amy's soul in the short time before its owner had departed into the darkness. But Menkhef was not sleeping now. He was in front of her, his lips brushing the shell of her ear as he spoke.

The teeth that had been nipping a line down the side of her throat paused, and her husband's familiar low chuckle puffed against her skin, making gooseflesh rise.

"I know exactly what she does to you," Elijah said, his chest pressing against her back. "She does the same damn thing to me. She always has."

Elijah's hand slid up to cup Amy's breast through the loose fabric of the shirt she was wearing. At the same time, he bit down on her neck, and her belly clenched as she felt the slide of razor-sharp fangs through skin. Menkhef made a small noise as though he'd been punched, and a second set of fangs pierced her neck on the other side. Her blood sang between them, base lust dragging a high-pitched, keening cry from her lips. She arched, trying to get *more more more*, and—

—a hand closed on her shoulder, shaking her gently from sleep.

"Ames, honey?" Elijah's voice held a thread of worry. "Come on, now. Wake up, you were having a nightmare."

She swallowed hard and blinked up at him, feeling her body still pressed up against the length of his in more or less the same position as when she'd drifted off.

"No," she rasped, her voice sleep-heavy and roughened by lust. "I really, *really* wasn't."

She tried to send her focus along the internal bond. Her connection with Elijah had seemed intermittent and unpredictable since Menkhef collapsed, as though he was the link they needed to reach each other properly. It must have done the trick, though, because Elijah's eyes widened, and he made a sound not dissimilar to the one Menkhef had made in the dream.

"*Jesus, Mary, and Joseph*, Ames," he said, "You're killing me, here."

She rolled upright and slung a leg over him, straddling her husband's lap so she could watch his face more closely. "You mean that," she said cautiously, not exactly a question, but not quite a statement, either. "It really doesn't bother you? It doesn't make you... angry, or disgusted with me?"

He pulled one of her hands away from his shoulder where she'd been using him for balance, and pressed her palm to his cheek instead— holding it there beneath his strong fingers. With the other hand, he grabbed her hip and slid her forward until she was centered over the hard, throbbing length of him.

"What do you think?" he asked, the same vulnerability she was feeling mirrored in the depths of his eyes.

"I don't know whose dream it was, Elijah," she whispered, feeling lost.

"What do you mean?" he asked, still cupping her hand against his cheek. Still holding eye contact.

"I mean," she said hesitantly, "this wasn't a memory. It wasn't Heqab and Nebetta, pictures from the past. It could just be... my stupid sex dream, you know? My subconscious getting its rocks off because you've been driving me crazy in all the best ways this past week."

Elijah's brows drew together. "I still don't understand. So what if it was just a stupid sex dream?"

She bit her lip, trying to put her worries into words. Her eyes wandered to the cot in the center of the room for a moment before returning to Elijah. "In some ways, we know everything about this man. But in others, we don't know him at all. He's so... distant, and unreadable, and just because we know how he felt about Nebetta and Heqab, it doesn't mean we know how he feels about *us*. He was kind to us. He protected us as best he could—

he saved our lives and kept the other vampires from turning us before we were ready. He managed to keep our child alive when he changed me. But... what if we're building up this big... thing... inside our heads that doesn't really exist?"

Elijah slid her hand down to his lips so he could kiss her palm. "I don't think we are, Ames. When I walked up those stairs from the South Tomb and the Light hit me..." He trailed off for a moment, clearing his throat. "When he caught me afterward and held me up... the way he spoke to me in my mind... well... I don't think that's the kind of thing you fake, just to be nice to someone."

But she only shook her head. "He also told us he wasn't the same person he used to be, and neither were we. He said if neither of us wished to be in his presence ever again, he'd understand."

Elijah just continued to watch her, his expression open and unguarded. "When he wakes up, I guess we'll just have to ask him."

When he wakes up.

"And when will that be?" she wondered bleakly.

-o-o-o-

The following morning, while Elijah was out doing who-knew-what in the neighboring village, Shay wandered in and made herself comfortable on the extra chair by Menkhef's bed.

"Um... hi?" Amy said, taken by surprise at the unexpected visit.

Shay smiled. "Hey, girl. Trynn said you needed to talk to me."

Amy blinked. "She did? I'm sorry, Shay—I don't know where she got that idea. I didn't say anything like that to her."

The other woman huffed a breath of amusement. "No, babe, you misunderstand. She didn't say you *asked* to talk to me. She said you *needed* to talk to me."

A bit of irritation crept in, though Amy tried to keep it out of her voice. "About…?"

"Relationships, I expect," Shay said matter-of-factly.

"*Excuse* me?" Amy nearly squeaked. "I'm sorry, but where do you—or Trynn, for that matter—get off inserting yourselves into other people's relationship issues without being asked?"

Shay only shrugged. "I get the impression that vamps aren't good with the whole *having boundaries* thing. A few people may have intimated over the years that I have a similar problem, so here I am, ready and willing to answer questions about having open and consensual relationships with more than one person at the same time."

With a jolt, Amy flashed back to the day of their arrival in Saqqara—resting in the shade with Elijah, only to have her eyes drawn to a trio of people laughing and talking nearby.

Shay must have seen the memory dawn, because she said, "Yup. *There* it is. I thought you'd remember eventually. You were practically slicing us open with invisible laser beams, you were staring at us so hard that day."

Shay's wide mouth was still quirked in a smile, but that didn't stop embarrassment from burning its way up Amy's neck to her cheeks. All of her irritation and defensiveness drained away, like a plug pulled in a bathtub.

"Oh, my god," she said, scrubbing a hand down her face. "I am *so sorry*, Shay. Both for then and for just now."

Shay snorted. "It's all right, on both counts. Believe me when I say that when you're part of a bisexual poly trio, you get used to people staring at you pretty fast. And for what it's worth, Trynn totally *is* meddling—but only because you so obviously need the help."

Amy took that on board for a moment or two before replying, "Okay... but I'm afraid I really have no idea what she expects me to ask, or want to talk about."

"Maybe you just need someone to say, 'Hey, polyamory is a real thing in the world and people do it all the time'?"

A short bark of laughter slipped past Amy's control. "Oh, wow. I can't believe I'm actually having this conversation. Holy shit." She ran a hand over her face. "Right, so how much do you know about my life? Or maybe I should ask how much Trynn knows about my life... only I'm not sure I want the answer to that."

Shay cocked her head. "The vamps have been trying to fulfill a prophecy involving a Council of Thirteen, and the first eleven consisted of five obvious couples, with one really sad-looking guy left over. Then you and your husband show up and end up getting turned, after which you're both here watching over Super Sad Guy more-or-less around the clock for days on end." She huffed in amusement. "Rocket science, it is not."

At that moment, Amy really wanted the ability to sink straight through the stone floor, and she vowed to pester one of the older vampires to get serious about teaching her to shift form into mist as soon as possible. On the other hand, it was also kind of a relief to have someone to talk to about this subject. Someone besides Elijah, that is.

"Well," she admitted, "when you put it like that..."

"Yup," Shay agreed. "So, first question. Is your husband on board with this, or is he freaking out?"

Amy scrubbed at her eyes, trying to get all the scattered bits of her brain corralled in one place. "He seems... surprisingly on board with it, to be honest."

"Cool. Next question. Are *you* on board with it?"

Amy met her eyes squarely. "Shay — I have absolutely no fucking clue."

"Okay. Arguments against?"

Amy took a deep breath. "I'm scared that Elijah isn't really as on board with this as he seems."

"So you think he's lying?"

She shook her head adamantly. "No, it's not that. You know vampires have a kind of... telepathic thing with each other, right? I can tell that he really feels that way."

"So you're projecting, or maybe using him as an excuse to avoid looking at your own feelings?"

Ouch. "Uh... yeah. Maybe so."

"Right. Next objection?"

Amy thought for a moment. "What will other people think?"

Shay grinned. "That you're weird, possibly going to hell, and probably into all sorts of kinky sex shit. Now, tell me—are you honestly more worried over what people will think about you being with two men, as opposed to what they'll think about you *being a vampire*?"

"Fair point," Amy mumbled.

"I'd say so. Next objection?"

Amy's eyes slid to Menkhef's face, peaceful in repose. "We have no idea how he really feels about us. He's... not exactly an easy one to read, and that's when he's *awake*."

"See, now—that's a valid objection. So, wait for him to wake up and ask him."

Amy wrinkled her nose. "Now you're starting to sound like Elijah."

Shay shrugged, a 'what can you do?' gesture. "Moving on. Arguments in favor?"

Amy sighed. "Elijah and I suck at being married on our own, and we've had dreams about him. Somehow that doesn't seem like a very good foundation for a serious relationship. Or even a seriously *weird* relationship."

Shay hummed thoughtfully. "Hmm, yeah. Maybe not. Still... the poor guy. I feel for him, you know? Stuck here all by his lonesome, while his other vampire buddies are happily paired off."

She reached out a hand as though to brush Menkhef's hair away from his forehead. Before the intent to move even registered in her mind, Amy had the other woman by the wrist, fangs erupting into points and her eyes burning in that way she knew meant they were glowing with an unearthly green light.

Shay met Amy's eyes with a very pointed — and a very *knowing* — look.

"*Oh my god.*" Amy realized what she was doing and dropped Shay's wrist like it had suddenly become red hot. She stumbled back a step, nearly falling over her upturned chair as she tried to put distance between herself and the defenseless human she'd just grabbed.

The defenseless human in question wriggled her fingers to restore the blood flow and tilted her head meaningfully. "Uh-huh. Thought so. Are you gonna make me spell it out, or have you got the memo now?"

"I've got the memo now," Amy said in a tiny voice. "Thank you, Shay."

"Don't mention it, babe," Shay said kindly. "If you're hungry later, I think Jason and Monique are on tap tonight. And if you get tired of waiting on Mister 'Walks Like a Pharaoh' over there—" She hooked a thumb at Menkhef. "—you might try the Prince Charming routine on him. You never know, right? If nothing else, he probably won't be expecting it."

To Amy's complete shock, Shay gave her a friendly hug on her way out — evidently unfazed by Amy's Bride of Dracula impersonation only moments before. Amy hugged her back gingerly. When she was alone again, she righted the chair and sank into it, her mind finally ditching its fruitless hamster wheel in favor of careening off in new directions… exploring new possibilities.

TWENTY-SIX

That evening when Amy went outside to help the others for a few hours, she made a point of tracking Trynn down. The other woman was at the Imhotep Museum, trying to hook the computer system there into a satellite phone link that had seemed to have a decent data connection earlier in the day.

Deciding to take a page from the other vampires' directness, Amy plopped down in a chair across the desk from where Trynn was scowling at her monitor screen and cleared her throat.

"Just a sec," Trynn muttered, not looking up as her fingers flew across the keyboard. "I need to finish this up and then devise some sort of terrible payback for Xander and that pimply IT kid of his. 'Why don't you just devise a protocol to let the computer systems piggyback on the satellite phone connection?'" She parroted in a decent impression of a British accent. "'Then maybe we can get a fast enough internet speed to be useful.' Because, *hey*, sounds simple, right?"

She continued to grumble at a lower volume while Amy sat waiting, her lips pursed to keep them from twitching. Eventually, Trynn sat back and stretched, cracking her knuckles.

"Any luck?" Amy asked.

Trynn's mouth twisted down. "Everyone and their dog who still has access to power and a working sat-phone is trying to use this link at once. Getting data through in either direction is like trying to pour molasses through a pinhole." She sighed. "So, what can I do for you? There isn't really anything here at the museum that would benefit from a second person, though I think Eris and Oksana were planning on moving more of the solar panels over here later."

"I talked to Shay," Amy said without preamble.

Trynn leaned back in her chair, finally giving Amy her full attention. "Oh, yeah? How'd that go?"

"I grabbed her by the wrist and flashed fangs at her when she tried to touch Menkhef," Amy said.

A furrow formed between Trynn's eyebrows. "Well, I did warn her your instincts might still be a bit heightened."

Amy's voice turned rueful. "I think she was counting on it."

Trynn's expression smoothed out. "No real harm done, then?"

"One of the legs on my chair is loose now, since I shoved it over. And I... might've left a bruise on her arm, though she didn't say anything about it, if so."

A shrug. "Could've been worse."

"She said you sent her," Amy said.

"Yup."

"Why? Why not come yourself?"

Trynn examined her for a long moment, as though choosing her words. "I'm not sure how much I could have helped you. I don't know Jack about dating multiple partners, and I have kind of a deep-seated *oh-god-no* reaction when it comes to picturing Snag romantically. I mean, er, picturing *Menkhef* romantically."

Amy scowled. "What's that supposed to mean?"

Trynn threw up her hands in the universal gesture for peace. "It's not supposed to mean anything. My mind just doesn't really want to go there. He's… well… he's *Snag*. That's all."

Amy stared at her, thinking of the stunningly statuesque specimen of male beauty currently resting on the cot in the South Tomb, silver hair streaking his temples, and tiny crows feet at the corners of his eyes. *Are you crazy, girl?* she thought in disbelief, before realizing that she didn't actually *want* other women lusting over Menkhef.

Or thinking about him in a romantic context.

Or, y'know, looking at him.

Shit.

Trynn laughed, and Amy covered her face with her hand and groaned as she remembered that Trynn could probably hear every one of those thoughts.

"Don't worry about it," she said kindly. "Here's the thing. You're still thinking like a human."

"Up until a week ago, I *was* a human," Amy pointed out.

"Yes," Trynn agreed. "And now you're a vampire. You're sitting there thinking, 'I barely know this crazy ancient Egyptian dude; how am I supposed to date someone who watched the pyramids being built?'"

"Er... yeah. Kind of?" Amy agreed.

"But that's the thing. You're not dating him, Amy. You're *mated* to him. You and Elijah both, I guess, and that's the part where Shay can be more helpful than I can."

"What does that even *mean*, though?" Amy asked, a plaintive note creeping into her voice.

Trynn met her gaze evenly. "It means your instincts go crazy at the thought of another woman so much as looking at your men. It means the idea of walking away, of being without them, makes you want to panic and tear the world apart with how wrong that is. It means that without them, you can never be a whole person. And without you, they can never be whole, either. It means that in the end, even death wasn't enough to keep you apart."

A lump rose in Amy's throat, trying to choke her.

Trynn's smile was lopsided and wistful. "Yeah, you understand what I mean. I can tell. Why don't you take the evening off and go back to the South Tomb? I'll let the others know. It's past time for the old scarecrow to wake up and help you and Elijah get this stuff figured out."

Amy nodded slowly, and rose.

"Why do some of you call him Snag?" she asked, aware that it was a non sequitur.

Trynn let out a low laugh and raised a finger, indicating her left canine. "Snaggle tooth, get it?" Her eyes crinkled at the corners. "I nearly lost my shit when I found out you were an dentist. You three need to get this worked out, because my life will *not* be complete until I've seen what Invisalign for vampires looks like."

Amy tried to swallow choked laughter for a moment before giving up and letting it out. The tension shattered, and she wiped wetness from her eyes. "Right. If I needed additional motivation, I guess I've got it now. Thanks for that—*I think.*"

The other woman grinned. "All part of the service. Now get out of here, and let me plot my revenge on uppity Brits who have no appreciation for the complexity of cross-platform programming."

"I'm going," Amy said. "When Menkhef wakes up, I'll let him know that you're angling to get him in my dentist's chair."

"You do that," Trynn said, and turned back to her code.

Amy left the museum and centered herself, intending to take the fast way back to the complex. She was a complete dunce when it came to transforming into mist, but she'd managed her owl form a few times now without anything disastrous happening. She closed her eyes, taking mental inventory of the clothes and personal items she needed to keep track of, and focused on becoming her avian avatar.

A moment later, she pushed off clumsily, flapping upward into the evening sky. The South Tomb was only moments away by air, as long as she avoided the distraction of scurrying mice and other tiny night creatures along the way. She fluttered back to earth on top of the cobra head wall, unwilling to test her flying skills in the narrow tunnels below. Another transformation, followed by a quick check to make sure she was still fully clothed, and she was jogging lightly down the stairs leading underground.

Elijah looked up in surprise when she appeared in the doorway and entered, closing the door behind her on creaking hinges. He rose to meet her, giving her a warm kiss before he spoke.

"Everything okay, sweetheart? I didn't expect you back for hours yet."

"Nothing's wrong," she assured him. "I'm just done with waiting for answers. I want to try something."

He looked at her curiously. "Try what?"

"The Prince Charming routine. Shay suggested it this morning."

"The… what, now?" Elijah gave her an odd look.

Amy huffed. "Sleeping Beauty? Prince Charming?" He still looked blank, and she rolled her eyes. "*I'm going to kiss him,*" she spelled out. "Assuming… you're okay with that?"

The words trailed off in a question.

Elijah stared at her. "Amy, since I've indicated on multiple occasions now that I find the idea of you having sex with him hot, I think you can take it as read that I'm not going to freak out over the idea of you kissing him."

She swallowed her embarrassment over doubting him yet again, when he'd clearly been signaling all along that he was open to exploring... whatever this turned out to be. *Projection*, Shay had called it.

So, was Amy really ready to do this?

Yes, she decided. Yes, she most certainly was.

"Sorry," she told Elijah. "That's my nerves talking. Up until now, this was all theoretical... but shit's about to get real, I guess."

"I think it's past time," Elijah said mildly.

She kissed him again, pouring all of her feelings into the slide of lips, and he returned those feelings a hundredfold.

"Love you, Ames," he said when he pulled back. A smile quirked his sensuous mouth as he continued, "And if you kiss him like that, he'd have to be a dead man not to respond."

Something fluttered low in Amy's stomach. "God, I love you so much," she said. "No matter what else happens, I'll always be yours. You know that, right?"

He ran his fingertips down her cheek. "We'll be each other's. I get that now, Amy. I understand what it means. Love's not a zero-sum game."

She pressed her face into his hand like a cat, closing her eyes for a long moment as she let those words sink in. "Yeah," she agreed.

Elijah nudged her toward the cot, and by unspoken agreement, they perched on opposite sides of the mattress — Amy on Menkhef's right, and Elijah on his left. Amy stared down at his still features for a long time, tracing them first with her eyes, and then with the tips of her fingers. He was so...

fucking... *regal*. It made him seem unapproachable. It also gave her a nearly overwhelming urge to muss him up a bit. To do something that would break through that cool reserve. She leaned down, teasing his lips with the faintest brush of hers.

Something stirred in the back of her mind — quiet and deep.

She kissed him again. It was like kissing a statue... right up until the moment when the statue kissed her back. A tiny movement; the merest slide of cool skin against hers. But that depthless presence inside her head roused further, coming slowly to life after long days of quiescence.

Amy closed her eyes, sinking into the mental connection even as she sank deeper into the kiss. A hand threaded into her curls and fisted, the gentle tug on her scalp zapping down the length of her spine like a lightning bolt and drawing a mewl from her lips. For a moment, she thought it must be Elijah, but she knew the feel of Elijah's hands.

This wasn't him.

Want spiraled higher, lengthening Amy's fangs. She was still unpracticed at managing the dangerous points, and the edge of her tongue rasped over the right one, opening a small wound. Menkhef made a low, male noise that did very interesting things to Amy's libido, and then he was holding her in place with both hands, demanding entrance to her mouth and tempting her tongue to explore his.

He sucked on it, drawing on the tiny cut... pulling her blood into him. The sensation made her toes curl, and she realized that she was grasping his shoulders so tightly that her fingernails were in danger of breaking his skin and drawing blood in turn. Deliciously wanton visions of tearing her mouth away so she could lick up every last drop threatened to unravel her control and distract her from the most important fact.

It had worked. He was awake.

Menkhef had risen to a seated position as they kissed, never relinquishing his grip on her or easing the exquisite ravishment of her mouth. Amy didn't think she had the strength of will to try and stop him, either. Especially not when she was getting echoes across the bond from a bottomless well of desire and raw need lurking in that powerful, ancient mind.

It was the kind of need that could devour someone whole, and leave them feeling grateful afterward for the opportunity to be consumed. So, it was honestly a disappointment as well as a relief when Elijah said, "Hey, old man. You know that's my wife you're kissing, right?"

Menkhef froze, his powerful aura furling up like a great bird of prey folding its wings. He pulled away from Amy's lips very carefully, his grip in her hair loosening.

Elijah's lips twitched as he continued, "Because I thought you might want to know, she loves it when you bite her lower lip. Though, mind you, I haven't tried it with fangs yet."

The tension in Menkhef's frame eased incrementally, and his brows drew together in something that looked like consternation.

"Guardsman," he said mildly, "are you *teasing me*?"

Elijah nodded. "Yup. And if you don't want it to become a regular thing, you'll probably need to work on your reaction—because right now it's priceless. So… welcome back. How are you feeling? Shall I get Mason in here to take a look at you?"

Menkhef blinked, as though he were just now cataloguing his surroundings and putting everything together in his head. His hand slid out of Amy's hair completely, and she tried not to mourn the loss. There were things they needed to discuss first. Questions that needed answers.

"I am… well," Menkhef said slowly, sounding like a man who also had questions he wanted answered.

"You've been asleep for seven days," Amy said, cringing a bit when it came out sounding like an accusation. She continued in a gentler tone. "We were worried."

His dark eyes softened. "It was not my intention to worry you." His brow twitched. "Nor was it my intention to sleep for seven days. That is… new."

"Hmm," Elijah said, leaning back to brace a hand behind him on the mattress. "Maybe try doing it in moderation on a more regular basis, rather than once every… what was it? Sixteen hundred years?"

"Sound medical advice," Menkhef said, the words emerging distinctly dry. "Perhaps Mason's presence will not be necessary after all."

"Lots of things have been happening since the battle… or whatever you want to call it," Amy said, bringing the conversation back to more somber territory.

"Yes," Menkhef said, sobering immediately. A light caress inside her mind drew Amy's attention to the mental link. "May I see?"

She nodded, and felt a deft touch slide through her memories of the past week, and Elijah's, as well. It didn't take long.

"You've done well," Menkhef said quietly. "All of you. I regret that my incapacity took you and your husband away from more important tasks."

"The others had it under control," Elijah said. "If they'd needed more from us, we would have worked something out. But everyone in Saqqara who needs it has food, water, shelter, and sanitation. Honestly, until communications recover, there's not a lot more we can do."

"Some of the others have been discussing going into Cairo to check things out, since it's not far from here," Amy said. "Now that you're awake, they'll probably want to move forward with that plan."

He nodded. "Logical."

"And speaking of the others, we should let them know you're all right," Elijah added.

"They are aware," Menkhef said. "I've asked them to give us privacy for a bit longer. There are… things we must discuss."

This was the moment, and Amy felt nervous butterflies gather in her stomach. She shot a glance at Elijah, who somehow appeared far more sanguine than she felt.

"Yes," she said. "We have questions." But that wasn't exactly right. "Well, okay—to be more accurate, we have *a* question."

"Then ask it," Menkhef said evenly.

She took a deep breath, steeling herself. "There's been this huge buildup about... fated mates, finding each other across different lifetimes and being reunited to live happily ever after. But... the whole time Elijah and I have been grappling with that—coming to terms with it—we've had no way of knowing if you even want that kind of happily ever after. No idea what it would look like if you *did* want it. You loved Nebetta and Heqab. But that was more than four thousand years ago. You told us that we're all different people now. Your friends just seem to assume that it doesn't matter... that we can somehow slide in and fill the space left by lovers who died in the ancient past. The question is— would you even want us to try?"

Her palms itched with nervousness. She clenched her hands into fists, wondering when she'd become so invested in Menkhef's answer to the question. Hadn't she been the nervous one? The uncertain one?

Menkhef reached out to cradle her face, his expression falling into lines of long-felt yearning. "*Hayati*," he said, "After the kiss you just shared with me, you really need to ask me this?"

"Told you," Elijah murmured.

"Okay," Amy said, relief and nervousness and excitement for the future singing in her veins like wine. "Okay, so—we're doing this. I have no idea how we even start, but let's *do* this."

Elijah laughed, and Menkhef smiled like the sun coming out, tucking a wayward red curl over Amy's ear.

"Maybe we should start simply," Elijah said. "Is that hunger I can feel through the bond, old man? You haven't had any blood in more than a week."

Menkhef shrugged the question off. "It can wait; it's not important."

Elijah held his gaze, a sad smile playing around his lips. Amy couldn't look away from the two of them—handsome, and kind, and principled, and... hers?

"It *could* wait," Elijah said patiently, "but there's no earthly reason why it needs to. It's true that you shouldn't drink more than a mouthful from Amy, because of the baby. But I'm right here. I'm topped up on blood bags... and I'm offering. I can always refill later."

"He can, you know," Amy said, her heart swelling until she thought it might burst. "I heard through the grapevine that Jason and Monique are on tap tonight."

"See? There you have it," Elijah said cheerfully.

Some deeply felt emotion passed across Menkhef's face, and he drew Elijah forward with a hand cupped around the nape of his neck. "My guardsman," he said quietly, and rested his forehead against the crook of Elijah's shoulder for a long moment. "Always concerned with the needs of others, rather than your own."

Elijah, too, looked like he was fighting some strong emotion, and Amy felt an echo of what had passed between the two after Elijah emerged into Israfael's Light.

"Not anymore," he said. "Not when I can look after both at once."

"Good." With that single word, Menkhef gently tipped Elijah's chin back and slid his fangs into chocolate-colored skin, sealing his sensuous lips over the twin wounds and drinking deeply.

Elijah's eyes fluttered shut. Longing swept through Amy like wildfire, and she realized that there was no longer any rational reason to deny herself. She shuffled across the bed to kneel at Menkhef's side. Once there, she kissed her way up Elijah's shoulder and sank her fangs into the other side of his neck. He gasped, his arm snaking around her to hold her tight against him as the cool delight of his blood spilled into her mouth.

She wasn't truly hungry, and didn't draw on the wounds to pull more from him—but hunger wasn't the point. As his blood flowed into both of them, the bond between them flared. She felt what they felt; knew what they knew. The truth of their connection flooded her, along with their mutual commitment to move forward and forge a new life in this uncertain future.

The three of them had seen a prophecy fulfilled against all odds. They had survived an apocalypse and confronted the depths of their own souls. After weathering all of those things and

emerging alive to tell the tale, facing the future together was nothing to fear.

EPILOGUE

Al Ghorab Stables, Cairo, Egypt — one year later

Amy hummed in satisfaction and leaned back against the well-muscled chest behind her. The arm wrapped around her ribcage to steady her gentled its hold as she let her head fall back into the cradle of a strong shoulder.

The bedroom was quiet except for the soft slide of skin on skin. Lit only by the glow of the moon slanting through the wall of west-facing windows, it was a silver-limned oasis, tastefully if sparsely furnished with rich wood and sumptuous fabrics. The house sat on a dozen or so hectares of land at the western edge of the Nile floodplain, just beyond the southern reaches of the Cairo Metropolitan Area.

It was set back from the road, nestled among irrigated pastureland, with opulent stables off to one side. Menkhef had purchased the property nine months ago, stating that he'd always enjoyed working with horses and had not had the opportunity to indulge the passion since he'd been a young man. He'd acquired a small but select band of Arabian broodmares, along with a promising young stallion boasting bloodlines that harkened back to the earliest written breeding records.

It gave him something to do, he said, while she and Elijah were traveling back and forth to the United States to sort out their affairs. Amy had been thrilled. She'd been horse-crazy as a teenager, scrimping and saving every penny she could for riding lessons at the local barn. Now, on the days when she wasn't busy volunteering her dental services to the underprivileged in and around Cairo, she could often be found sneaking out for an hour to ride her fiery chestnut mare, or just to work in the barn, surrounded by the smell of hay and leather.

Elijah had given notice at his old teaching position in Pennsylvania, and landed a new post at the American University in Cairo, an English language institution with a well-respected archaeological program specializing in Egyptology. He'd returned to his first love—field research. But now, his digs were practically on his doorstep, an easy commute from their home overlooking the Western Desert.

And together, they lived.

The pace of their lives these days was busy, but not frantic, and for perhaps the first time in her life, Amy was at peace. She had everything that she needed. She knew why she was here, and how she could help make the world a better place with her presence.

Even though Menkhef—stubborn bastard that he was—still hadn't let her straighten his maloccluded canine.

But that was all right. Everyone needed fresh goals to aspire to... and besides, that particular snaggle tooth had kind of grown on her over the past year.

Lips nuzzled the sensitive skin beneath Amy's ear, and she shifted restlessly in Menkhef's lap. The movement jostled his hard length buried inside her, pressing against the spot on the front wall of her passage that made her inner muscles clench deliciously. Her breath huffed out, the rest of her body feeling soft and liquid after nearly a half-hour of his unhurried attention to her pleasure.

Her Egyptian lover was inhumanly patient in all things, and definitely in the matter of sex. She lived for the moments when she could pierce his much-vaunted control. Those moments were rare, but they could be volcanic in their intensity.

Tonight, she knew, would not be such a night. They were all feeling lazy, and their time right now was not unlimited. So, she was content to let the boys have their fun, and reap the benefits with a happy and grateful heart.

"Touch her," Elijah said from his comfortable sprawl in the chair next to the bed, where he was watching the show. "Make her come again."

As they always did, her husband's low-pitched suggestions ratcheted up her simmering desire, heating it to the boiling point. Knowing he was watching—knowing he was enjoying the show, getting off on her pleasure—it did things to her. Powerful things.

Menkhef slid one hand over her breasts, trailing it upward to rest over the arched expanse of her bared throat. It was a silent admonishment not to move—to remain pliant and loose in his embrace while he shattered her. She moaned, making no effort to lift her head from where it had fallen back to rest on his shoulder.

His other hand smoothed over her belly, fingers trailing past neatly trimmed pubic hair to delve into her folds and circle her clit. With a feeling like the tide coming in, her pleasure rose. Her muscles fluttered around his thick shaft, and he rolled his hips in an easy rhythm beneath her. He could have pushed her into a climax in mere moments, but even in this, he drew things out until she thought she might go mad.

She was considering the merits of shamelessly begging for mercy by the time the hand holding her throat tipped her head to one side. His fangs pierced her flesh, sliding deep. She cried out softly and came hard around his cock, the climax going on for so long that she wasn't sure if she was light-headed due to blood loss or orgasm exhaustion. Menkhef made an animal noise against the tender skin of her neck and came right along with her, drinking her blood in deep swallows as he did.

When they both came back to themselves and Amy dragged heavy eyelids open, it was to find Elijah watching them intently, one foot resting on the edge of the bed as he fisted his cock with slow, firm strokes.

"Nuh-uh," she said groggily. "Hands off. That's mine."

She was slurring a bit, but Elijah only smiled at her. He made a point of sliding his fist along the heavy length a few more times before letting his hand fall away.

"Greedy," he accused fondly.

She smirked, and pointedly turned her attention back to Menkhef, craning her head around until they could kiss, even though the angle was a bit awkward. She could taste her own blood on his tongue, and his as well, after he purposely scored his lip so she could suck on it. She carried on until she heard Elijah shift restlessly in his chair, and then broke away with a final tender brush against Menkhef's soft smile.

Amy slid free of his body and prowled toward the edge of the bed, her movements loose and sloppy with relaxation. The chair Elijah was sitting in had no arms, which made it easy to crawl into his lap, facing him, and impale herself on the impressive erection he'd been teasing her with earlier.

The feeling of being split open by a fresh, straining cock while her nerves were still oversensitive and singing from fucking her other lover had quickly become one of Amy's favorite things in life. She growled and wrenched Elijah's head back, not being gentle as she tore into his neck and rode him hard.

Elijah's hands grasped her buttocks, strong arms lifting and lowering her onto his hot length as she drank him down. He came first, helpless beneath her onslaught, and the feel of it through the bond triggered her as well. It was like an earthquake—deep and far-reaching, leaving her slumped boneless in Elijah's arms.

Mere moments later, fussing noises came from the baby monitor on the bedside table, and Elijah chuckled into her hair. "Timing like an orchestra conductor," he murmured.

Amy snickered into his neck, just relieved that the unhappy cries hadn't started ten minutes ago.

I have her this time, Menkhef sent along the bond, already reaching down next to the bed to retrieve a pair of loose sleep pants. Amy let her silent thanks flow back to him, and kissed Elijah deeply before easing off of his body. He gave her ass a final companionable squeeze and lifted one hand to his mouth, yawning deeply.

"This is going to be a long day," he observed, and stretched. "Worth it, though."

Amy watched the play of muscles in moonlight with appreciation. "Definitely worth it," she agreed.

After cleaning up quickly and donning a robe, she returned to find Menkhef back in the room, cradling Neqaba against his bare chest as he looked down at her with a soft expression on his ageless features. His black hair had grown out until it fell over his shoulders in raven waves, and Amy took a moment to appreciate the picture he made with their daughter.

To appreciate what her life had somehow become.

She settled herself against the headboard of the bed and accepted the warm, squirming bundle into her arms. Neqaba squalled in distress, but it took her only a moment to realize where she was and latch onto Amy's nipple. Amy cooed to her and stroked her fingers over Neqaba's dark curls, wondering if it were possible to overdose on happy endorphins from breast-feeding while still high on mind-blowing sex and drinking blood.

Elijah chuckled and settled next to her on the bed. "Probably not," he said in response to her un-aired musing. "But if you feel like volunteering for a more in-depth study, I'm happy to participate."

She wrinkled her nose at him.

"How long until the others get here?" she asked, rather than replying to Elijah's teasing. "For some reason, I seem to have completely lost track of time. No idea how that happened."

"Two hours or so," Menkhef replied, perching on the edge of the bed to watch their child nurse.

Amy yawned. "Okay. Two hours—that's doable. I definitely need a shower first, though. And frankly, so do both of you."

Elijah drew breath to say something, and she cut him off.

"*Separate* showers. Or the two hours suddenly becomes way less doable," she said sternly

Elijah shot Menkhef a rueful look. "Oh, well. You can't say I didn't try."

-o-o-o-

Eris and Trynn were the first to arrive that morning—unsurprising, since they, too, maintained a residence in Cairo. Trynn freelanced, plying her computer skills to several clients including Xander's company, HelioTeque. Eris had dusted off a couple of academic degrees and attached himself to Al Azhar University, one of the oldest institutions of higher learning in the world. He and Trynn were relatively frequent visitors to the house, and one or both of them usually had a virtual chess game going with Menkhef via email at any given time.

Tré and Della were next, with eleven-year-old Allison in tow. While both Amy and Elijah's immediate families had escaped harm during the events a year ago, Della's family had not been so lucky. Her mother had survived, and Della had sought her out shortly afterward to let her know she was still alive and explain what had happened. Della's estranged father had been killed, however, as had her aunt and uncle—Allison's parents. The little girl had been injured badly, but survived. Della and her mate had taken her in immediately upon finding out about the tragedy.

Manisha and Xander showed up shortly thereafter. They were living in London, to no one's very great surprise. Manisha was pursuing an advanced psychology degree with an eye toward trauma counseling, while Xander continued to expand his renewable energy company. Amy had learned that while all of the original vampires held a fair amount of personal wealth accumulated simply by virtue of investing money over the course of several lifetimes, it was Xander's company that allowed them to truly not have to worry about anything. He distributed the profits freely among his friends, seemingly unconcerned that none of them except Trynn contributed to the business in any meaningful way.

The final group to arrive was a boisterous one. Mason, Oksana, Duchess, and Chan had traveled together from Haiti, along with Oksana and Mason's brood of adopted Haitian children. There were four of them—all boys—ranging in age from seven to sixteen. The youngest, Cristofer, looked at Mason in particular with hero-worship in his eyes, and the oldest, Eniel, had always seemed to have wisdom far beyond his years. *An old soul*, Oksana would observe with a smile, ruffling his hair.

Mason and Oksana had returned to the island to continue Mason's previous work, this time with private funding that allowed them to get the resources they really needed. Amy was a bit in awe of the pair—they were making a tremendous difference for the war-torn country's orphans and child soldiers.

Duchess and Chan had been helping them for the past several months. What had started out as a way to stay busy and be productive while they decided on a long-term plan had, Amy suspected, become their passion as much as it was Oksana and Mason's. She was glad; Amy liked the idea of them being together. This was such an odd, close-knit group—it only seemed right that they would gravitate together, the same way Eris and Trynn had gravitated toward Cairo.

After hugs and greetings had been exchanged, Amy made sure that all the children were fed and had a chance to freshen up. Then Elijah sent them to the stables to greet the horses under the watchful eye of Ahmed, the farm manager.

Menkhef had set up tables and chairs on the east-facing patio, a pleasant space enclosed by a low stucco wall, and partially covered by an overhead trellis from which hung a riot of flowering vines. A faint wash of pink and orange was just starting to tint the sky above the horizon, heralding dawn's approach.

They made themselves comfortable in the cool predawn, easy together as only people who truly understand each other can be.

"It hardly seems as though a year has passed," Xander mused, leaning back with his ankles crossed in front of him.

"Speak for yourself, mate," Mason said wryly. "I hardly feel as though I've had time to stop and breathe in the past twelve months."

"Which is just the way you like it," Oksana said.

Mason shrugged and didn't deny it. "Maybe so." He smiled at Amy, who held Neqaba cradled in her arms, sleeping soundly. "How's the sprog doing these days, Amy? Looks like she's growing by leaps and bounds."

Amy couldn't help the radiant smile that blossomed on her face. "She's doing well, Mason. Healthy and happy, thanks to you."

Amy had been on tenterhooks through her entire pregnancy; terrified that something would go wrong. Neqaba had clung to her vampire mother's womb tenaciously and been born without incident, only to suffer terrible colic and slow weight gain afterward. Amy had discovered ahead of time that her milk was tainted with blood in the same way that vampire tears and other bodily fluids were, so they'd made the decision to put Neqaba on formula immediately. It had been Mason who'd realized that Amy's milk might be exactly what her daughter needed, and to everyone's surprise and relief, the tiny infant had thrived on the pink-tinged liquid her breasts produced.

No one knew exactly what Neqaba was... vampire, human, or something in between. To their knowledge, there had never been another baby like her. As far as Amy was concerned, though, as long as she grew up healthy and happy, it didn't matter. She was Neqaba. She was Amy's daughter. The rest could take care of itself.

"I'm glad to hear it," Mason said, still gazing at the little girl with a fond smile.

Amy smiled as well, trailing a fingertip over Neqaba's soft cheek.

Many things had changed. The world a year after Israfael's final confrontation with Bael was a place experiencing both lingering trauma and burgeoning hope. The official death toll had eventually come in at almost two hundred seventeen million people worldwide, a figure that was both heartbreaking and impossible to truly grasp.

Aside from Della's family members, the vampires had mourned the loss of Mason's elderly mother in Australia, Elijah's faculty supervisor at West Parklands University, a friend named Madame Francine in New Orleans, and several of Xander's employees in both London and Romania.

It had been so random, and so utterly, completely pointless. For months, Amy had worried that the worst parts of human nature would take over, plunging the world into dark times. But while there were certainly moments of darkness, more people seemed to have gained a new appreciation for life and love after the terrifying months when Bael gained sway over the world.

The destruction and death had decimated the economy, but people were building it up again—making better decisions and looking toward a brighter future. As a group, the vampires had made a valiant effort at keeping a low profile, occasionally by means of a bit of hypnotic influence aimed at reporters or other humans who got too close or too pushy. As time went on, the public's attention moved to other things, as it is wont to do.

"Look. The sun's coming up," Chan said quietly.

By unspoken accord, Amy rose with the others and went to stand by the low wall bounding the eastern edge of the patio, Neqaba still asleep in her arms. Menkhef stood at her left side, and Elijah, at her right. The others joined them, standing shoulder to shoulder as the first sliver of brilliant orange light illuminated the horizon, brightening the eastern sky from navy blue to turquoise.

The fiery orb slid higher, bathing them in liquid warmth that turned everything gold. Amy watched as Menkhef closed his eyes, lifting his face toward the glowing rays. Elijah's arm slid around her waist, pressing her against his side.

Ahead of them, a new day dawned.

finis

Thank you for reading the *Circle of Blood* series. R.A. Steffan and Jaelynn Woolf are also collaborating on *The Last Vampire: Book One.*